Cheers!
Many thanks for
the support!

TO TIRE OF REST

"I think it's time we try again," said the Mother. She lay on the leaves of the Island of Autumn, her head pillowed by a root.

The Father was grieved. "It went so poorly before, and how much more can we give? Isn't it enough to care for the colours, and to shepherd the ways of sleep?"

"What is cost," she replied, "but another part of the cycle? It won't hurt forever."

"I..." he began, but did not know how to begin.

Her smile was like a drift of snow. Glistening, elegant, calm. Winter was not their domain, but the Island of Autumn was not without snow. A drift, like her smile, had a lopsided curve. It was heavier than it looked, showed up well in a picture, but could cover ever so much loss.

And you could make anything out of it, with intention and determination.

He sighed, and she turned her face and braced herself. Was he weary for her sake, for what she would carve out of herself so that others might make their own carvings? Or was it exhaustion, spiritual and sublime, from toiling to guide those who mistook burrowing for growth?

"I'll need your help," he said, as he opened her wounds to hope.

Butterflies emerged in answer. Each of them a universe, blessed with transformation, and hopeless distances of emptiness. Every movement was as much a flutter as a sheen, and they went on to become and to having been.

Author's note: *This flash fiction piece won the December 2019 Kit Sora Flash Fiction Contest. Run by Engen Books, this contest invites authors to submit pieces of 250 words or less to be inspired by or paired with an image created by the luminous photographer, Kit Sora. If you haven't already checked out her* Artobiography, *drop everything and go do so. My book will still be here when you get back.*

Published in Canada by Engen Books, St. John's, NL.

Library and Archives Canada Cataloguing in Publication information is available on the publisher's website.

ISBN-13: 978-1-77478-089-3

Distributed by:
Engen Books
www.engenbooks.com
submissions@engenbooks.com

First mass market paperback printing: March 2022

Cover Image: Mandi Coates
Cover Design: Ellen Curtis

INTERSTITCHES
WORLDS SEWN TOGETHER

MATTHEW DANIELS

SAFE GUARD

Here's how it works: turn with the clock. Enter a number. Your next turn is against the clock, which should tell you a lot. It doesn't. But then you get to move with the clock again. There you have it.

Here's why that matters: you couldn't possibly look after matters yourself. Money? Give it to a bank. Health decisions? It's the doctor's office for you. Can't take the pressure? Lock it in a bottle, Captain Morgan will look after it. If work is in your way, give it to time. Tomorrow will keep it safe.

And now, here you are: locking your papers behind walls with an armored door. Safe. Easily recognized, it declares, "I'm hiding something valuable." Belief in the strength of its walls begins and ends with that dial.

Strength in numbers.

You always wanted the name Garrison, but people generally don't get to handle their own names. To be fair, what can you do? Go by a number until you're old enough to realize the importance of a name? And then people have to re-learn who you are? Much easier just to name your son Garrison.

Garrison never cared much for the bottle. He'd stick a straw in an apple for juice if it worked that way. But money? Too many numbers. It wasn't safe. So he trusted another box with spinning figures. Just put his money in, pull a lever, and wait for easier times.

Your grandson doesn't know much about you. Garrison never calls, never visits, so little Robin doesn't get much chance. Doesn't matter. You've seen him grow. Strong one, swift as cash registers. Doesn't know his father's birthday. You're not going to be the one to tell him. He kept the drawing his father made for him when he was a boy. Couldn't have been more than three when he promised Garrison he'd fly, just like the bird in the drawing.

And that's how it is. Big future. Garrison tried to help, only way he knew how. Back to his box, pay for the boy's tuition with clinking piles of chance. Robin's not worried. He's got a swimming scholarship. Has a future so big, he can't lift it himself. So he's going to give it to the university. Have it pressed into paper and gold letters.

Enter his numbers. Street, apartment, social insurance, phone, course. Turns with the clock, caught up and fast. Next? Age, deadlines, loans for the walls. All of this is against the clock. Now the gold letters are keeping him from a job. No work in the field, no one to pay his weight in paper and potential. But he keeps digging, turning with the clock. He'll dig out that future with his bare hands if he has to.

Scratch and win.

To my marvelous grandmother,
Winnifred "Winnie" Daniels.
You brought together more than you know.

FROZEN ORBIT

The Moon was an afterthought.

Cyril's mission was the station, woven into the sky of the Moon with threads of mathematics and ambition. Well, and a great deal of money. From here, the Moon was just a monstrous grey rock that had taken blistering punishment. He could relate.

He was here for gravity studies. His mission was falling. There were others in the project, but space had a way of spreading all that out. Even the words were farther away. He'd play recordings of epic poetry while he ventured into labyrinths and dark forests of calculations, psychological analysis, fuels, rockets. Seals. Everything was airtight. Doors were seamless. A window was less wind than shield.

It was Earth that had been the escape. Blue was a celestial lie, made out of water vapor like smoke and light being torn up by the atmosphere. The sky was a mirror with teeth. Out here, there was no smoke. Only the telescopes had mirrors.

Cyril wanted a Neil Armstrong legacy. Like an epic

poem with a single line, he wanted to be both swept away in a moment and immortalized. Mining stars, building artificial worlds, speaking with people born without tongues. Sailing darkness.

Below, the Moon stayed the same. Sometimes pockmarked, sometimes plain, he'd seen enough of it to forget it was there. Earth was more interesting. A moon that was new, at least to him.

Jokes helped with the paperwork. Crew conversations, videos from home, singing with recordings. Singing with machines, with imagination. Singing with the silence. It kept the numbers from chewing on him while he worked. He rarely got in on the arguments, though. This wasn't about the triumphs of humanity or saving the species.

Cyril, in fact, had a hard time telling people why he chose to be so far away from humanity. There were no dramatic plane crashes. He'd learned aerodynamics in class, not from the handheld objects of drunken parents. "What can I say? I guess I'm a lunatic!"

It wasn't high adventure or fear of the mundane.

He just had to pull the wires out of the sky.

The Moon was an afterthought.

Author's Note: *This piece was shortlisted for the Cambridge Flash Fiction Prize 2021, from TSS Publishing. For more, check out* https://theshortstory.co.uk/competitions/short-story-competition/ff-results/

TABLE OF CONTENTS

DAY THREE

She builds rockets.

Not the NASA ones, though. The passengers are not satellites, not garbage. Human in a way, but not always kind. Little more than Legos will fit, perhaps a letter to love or hope. It's a hobby. She's been doing it since she was young. Now she's middle-aged, which is more romantic than the promise of youth. It's when we see those promises being kept.

She's an event coordinator. She has people drinking gossip and trading coffee. All the languages of marketing and keeping the peace.

She likes to call launch time Day Three, no matter the date. Her family thinks it's because she was diagnosed on the third visit.

It's because they told her they loved her on the third day of treatment.

She knows the sickness and cannot change its name.

Textbooks discuss how it makes the patient weak. Beds, timelines, times, and bed lines.

"Is it contagious?" is the question she gets asked the

most.

People.

Honestly.

There's a soccer field. You can see it from the hospital. She used to go there herself, but now she has to watch the launches from the window. Coordinating them over the phone. Called a cell; a prison when you can only move your voice.

"It's Day Three," she says to the nurse. "What'll I have them put in it?"

The nurse says, "I didn't know you put things in them."

She smiles because it is an image of strength.

"Have you tried hope?" the nurse asks while making adjustments and taking notes.

"Once," she answers.

PAGE 0 OF

Menefer opened her eyes to the translucent greenish-yellow lid of her capsule. There was some pain in the right side of her neck, but odd aches and pains were common when coming out of cryo-sleep. She lifted the journal that she'd taken with her into slumber. Paper records were uncommon these days, but she liked the feel of them. Even before opening the capsule, she opened the book. Empty. This journal was fresh.

"There aren't enough stars," Menefer wrote before she got up.

It was a personal motto of hers, and not as negative as it seemed; there weren't enough stars to stop her, or to explore. Every fresh journal got that as the first entry.

She was alone in the dormitory. By itself, that wasn't unusual; the crew of the spacecraft were much more industrious than she was. Her biggest job, it seemed, was guilt: she'd built this ship. Not literally, of course, but she'd made faster-than-light travel (FTL) a reality.

Next to her capsule was a storage unit for her personal effects. She received no special treatment beyond research access and asked for none, so the unit was standard issue: eight feet tall, two feet wide, and equipped with adjustable fittings like hooks and shelves. The rest of the vessel would be supplied with everything the ship's crew and passenger required, so this storage provision was for the truly personal; family photos, sports gear, collectibles such as books, and even blankets were common. Practical and uniform clothing was provided, but everyone kept clothing that felt more human. Many used accessories or jewellery, rather than abandoning the uniform entirely.

Menefer chose oversized sweaters.

She often kept her focus narrow these days. She'd look at her own capsule as she got out of it. Alongside the military green metallic storage unit, the cream-coloured cylinder with greenish-yellow lid resembled a bizarre battery setup. Menefer never stepped back to take them all in; it made everyone and their units look like resources. Plugged in. Ready for consumption.

After her ablutions — morning exercise, nutritional paste, supplements, cleaning, and the like — Menefer grabbed her journal. Jotting down her thoughts as she went helped to keep the guilt away. She stepped into the corridor leading to what everyone called the Engine Room.

All the walls, including those of the dormitory, had the same panelling. Interspersed among them were structures for maintenance, communication, measurement, tools, equipment, and so forth. When deactivated, the panels looked like ceramic with a clear glass overlay. Generally, they projected all manner of imagery and information: time of day (programmed to be consistent with the local time of the launch site in India on Earth), ship status, special reports, location in the interstellar medium, and various other details Menefer noted instead of thinking about her invention.

No one had (yet) passed her by. That was not unusual, and she worked on not thinking about the reason for it. So accustomed was she to writing in her journal that she could do so without looking down at it. She usually only glanced at it to see what she'd written so far, or to consult an earlier note.

"The universe, according to cosmology and quantum theory, relies upon an observer. If the relationship between observer and universe could be either intensified, reduced, or altered, then the difficulties of FTL..."

Menefer closed her journal, took a breath, and opened it to a clear page.

Think: she hadn't seen the crew yet.

Think: she had her journal. She'd need somewhere to sit. The Engine room was equipped with seating, as she spent most of her time there, studying and examining the technology she'd —

No!

Dormitory.

Halls. Yes, she could think of those. Consistent. They liked consistency here, though they had their parties and spontaneity. Today the panelling had been programmed to look like the inside of an aquarium. The panels themselves served as the glass casing, and the imagery became whatever lived inside. They extended into a formless aquamarine distance. There was a blue whale.

There were manta rays, many schools of silvery or

multi-coloured fish, and seafloors that extended into unknown depths after a comfortable distance. Menefer watched the whale. It was a living monument, and her primal mind made her think it was the same size as the stars or nebulae she could see if she set the display differently.

One of the crewmembers had once set a room to display the ship's actual surroundings in space, despite the warnings. He'd needed a month of mental health treatment. Most assumed that planets, stars, glorious clouds of space dust, asteroid fields, and so on would be right there. Most people — even if they knew it as a concept — didn't really feel how vast it was out here. At some points in their journey, there had been nothing but the faint twinkle of distant stars to tell them that they weren't in an endless black void.

Hence the display panels.

Entering the Engine Room always felt like a breach. Was it because she didn't want to have to contend with herself and her thoughts, or was she stepping into Aspen's private space?

"Subject Aspen's condition is nominal," she wrote as she inspected the monitors. Menefer watched the Engine. It was a heavily modified medical capsule containing a man in his sixties. He'd been chosen because he was in the middle stages of Alzheimer's disease. The programmable panelling of the Engine Room was usually set to stark and clinical whites or greys, with accents of pastel colours designed to soothe anyone who entered the room. The Engine was both quiet and disquieting.

Aside from Aspen's life support and the machinery

for the FTL drive — mostly blocky hardware and bright, coloured tubes that played off the pastel tiles — the only furnishing in the room was an elaborate observation and control station. Menefer took the single seat. There were buildings with less elaborate architecture; it was intended to last for decades and provide optimal ergonomic support, in addition to innumerable control options and conveniences.

The act of sitting automatically caused the odd framing in front of the plush-looking seat to produce a split hologram. From her position, the left side of the room became a black background with silvery grey fonts. They gave a full readout of Aspen's physical and mental status, as well as the Engine's functions and all the information related to how the Engine connected to the ship.

On her right, split from the left by a blurry line of stark white, was the image of a classical home. Yellow walls with chocolate brown accents and, in the background, brown bannisters with a railing for the stairs to the second floor. There was a three-deep bookshelf furnished with a framed photograph, knick knacks, a plant on top, and even a few books. A curtained window. Hardwood floors. Aspen was in a rocking chair, arguing with a woman Menefer knew was a home care worker.

"His crisis is continuing," she wrote as she watched the Engine's numbers and Aspen's denial.

If you could be linked to a machine designed for observation on the scale of galactic gravity, then your observation of that very reality would start to matter. Menefer squeezed her eyes shut.

"It's worth it," she wrote.

Only dimly was she aware of the scratching of her shaky hand on the paper.

The whole room was an altar to his emotional turmoil. The crisis was critical; if there was some part of your reality you couldn't accept, if there was something unchangeable you broke your nails trying to change, then you put pressure on your observation of reality.

The machine then put that pressure on the observation of the laws of the universe.

Their ship didn't even need fuel, aside from powering the lights, computers, and life support. It was a ship propelled by pain. This was how they would get to other solar systems, galaxies, and deep space.

Menefer looked at the journal.

"It's worth it" was repeated on the page. Over and over. The letters got more and more scraggly, misaligned, and downward-angled.

Lifting her head with a gasp, she looked around the Engine Room. She was alone. Surveillance from outside the room was unnecessary; rigorous interviews and testing had ensured that no one on board would willingly compromise the vessel. Operations data were important, but they could be monitored from anywhere on the ship.

"Now that we're at speed…" she didn't realize she'd written that on a fresh page.

It didn't matter. She couldn't bear to put poor Aspen through this anymore. "Surely it can be slowed as we approach a planet. Can we really give humanity the stars by putting humans into a world of fire?"

The Engine had an interactive setting to ensure that a state of crisis was maintained. "Interfear," she wrote.

A tasteless joke. Hands shaking, she activated the holographics and spent hours trying to help Aspen come to terms with his Alzheimer's.

She was making progress.

The Engine began to shudder.

"I'll have to settle my affairs..." Aspen's image murmured. They were standing in an imitation of his hallway, next to the stairs. "I should thank you, I know, but I can't..."

The Engine's tremulous hum stung the bones.

Uniforms began stepping into the imagery.

"No!" Menefer shouted. "We can't do this to him anymore! I can keep up the momentum! You can't! Don't...!"

One of them jammed something into the right side of her neck. Her arguments became sloppy wet muscle. Darkness without stars.

Menefer opened her eyes to the translucent green lid of her capsule. There was some pain in the right side of her neck, but odd aches and pains were common when coming out of cryo-sleep. She lifted the journal that she'd taken with her into slumber. Paper records were uncommon these days, but she liked the feel of them. Even before opening the capsule, she opened the book. Empty. This journal was fresh.

COLOUR OF ZERO

Who'd have thought that emptiness could be baggage?

"Why do you even have that thing?" Piper demanded. She wore capris and a long-sleeved shirt. The sleeves should have been rolled up, but the gravity of desperation and water made them uneven. Her postcard was dissolving in a pocket.

Kieu was lunge-walking in the waist-high water. Her gold and purple skirt clung to her legs as the wind clung to the rest of her. On the surface of the water, translating the water's violence, was a yellow hard-backed suitcase. Both Kieu and the empty luggage were rags under a digging sky.

It tried to burrow into water, buildings, ground, and civilization. "We have twenty miles to go for real help!" Kieu shouted over the crashes of weather and failures of architecture. "We'll need to carry food!"

Obliged to help Kieu and her luggage of desperation, Piper cursed at the grocery store a block ahead of them. Torrential humanity threw aside its orderly designs and cascaded upon things that were nailed down, things that weren't, and things that could be weapons because of what once held them together.

Animals floated by, mechanical and no longer worried. The hurricane bled away all colour and the women were soaked in survival. All the people they could see were little more than part of the storm.

"It'll be harder to carry with food!" Piper shouted in dismay.

Kieu heard only the cold.

THE IRONY OF GLASS

Thatcher Verra drank from the limeade bottle in the cup holder attached to his office chair and waited for the other players of *Civilization VI* to make their moves. He had an assortment of online work, mostly freelance and various levels of legal, and was enjoying the break.

Crumb was winning.

There was a flicker from the window. Without bothering to stand, he simply wheeled his chair to the side of his robust entertainment setup. The computer was so large it was practically diesel-powered, with a plain black CPU tower and three monitors placed in a floor-to-ceiling shelf.

His window was at ground level. There was nothing immediately next to it, but there was a second flicker as something passed through the sunlight. As he approached, he saw that it was a rock dove. He liked to picture them with guitars, rocking out in studded leather jackets.

The rock dove half-flew and half-walked about the gravel at the base of the window, doing nothing intelligible. It flitted about three more times. Leaving the overweight Hispanic man with his computer, it took flight.

At first, it stayed above the street. There was not a single person. Two dogs were wandering about, and a cat lounged atop the hood of a Buick. The pigeon saw what it thought was a metal bird. It fled to one of its favourite feeding grounds: the town's hotel.

First it decided to perch on a branch. Before the tree was a large set of windows looking in on the reception desk. Standing at that desk was a pimply young man wearing a face mask. He'd just set aside his cleaning cloths and was talking to the woman before him.

"Hello and welcome to Towerton," the young man said. His nametag read Isaac. The woman made note of this, out of habit.

She smiled awkwardly, trying to hide the anxiety she couldn't place. "Er, hi. Thank you. Why are you wearing a mask?"

"Germs."

She frowned. "Is there something going around?"

"It's the time of year," he said. It was well into Spring at this point, but she didn't bother to pursue the question further. He followed with, "Can I help you?"

His voice was thin and strained, which was odd because of the muffling of the mask. The new arrival replied, "Yes, I had a reservation?"

As he turned to the computer at his station, the young man started nodding. It seemed to be subconscious, like a pensive person sticking out their tongue. "What was the name?"

"Meredith Heaney," she replied. She pronounced it with slightly more volume and distinction than her everyday speech, as though the name should hit home.

Isaac was nodding. "Room 57," he said, though she couldn't tell if he was talking to her or to himself. As he returned from the key boxes with the appropriate key, he handed her a cleaning cloth and moved the key towards the surface of the counter. Stopping, he blinked and flushed. "Here you go, ma'am," he said, correcting his configuration.

She smiled and brushed off the error. "Thank you," she said as she took it and he pointed in the direction she needed to go. "Oh," she added, and he stopped from picking up a spray bottle. "I would appreciate some help bringing in my personal effects. Would you...?"

His heart sank, but then he remembered. "Let me just page the assistant manager," he said. When she blinked in surprise, he added, "We have a new service she's been wanting to show off." Isaac seemed to brighten as he spoke, and Meredith detected relief in his tone, though she couldn't put a finger on why.

"I...uh...okay," she said.

It didn't take long for the assistant manager, a middle-aged Aboriginal woman, to show up. "Hello, hello," she chirped. "I'm Chantelle Naranja, delighted to meet you. I hear you'd like to see our new drone carriage service?"

Meredith made herself grin. "Why, yes." She hadn't mentioned her corporate background when she made the call. Had her name gotten ahead of her? Did one of her colleagues head her off?

Chantelle led Meredith to a sparsely furnished side room. A young man sat before a control terminal. "Stewart," the assistant manager began, "Please demonstrate for our guest how the new system works."

"Sure thing!" he said. Meredith cast a perfunctory glance over the control board, which included a display from a camera in flight.

"Now," Chantelle resumed, "Let's meet up with it!"

Feeling a little breathless, and unable to explain the prickling at the back of her neck, Meredith followed. After a brief stroll down a hallway, during which time they exchanged small talk, they arrived at a scene that made Meredith beam. Before her was a wall-height window, modified with something like an oversized mail slot.

"Meet Hummingbird," Chantelle grinned. Holding a stable flight on the other side of the window was, in fact, a drone. It had limbs added to the base model, so that it looked like a metal insect pretending to be a bird. The logo it sported featured an android head out of the eighties, shaped like a flying saucer with a white space for the visor. In that visor space was a font designed to look like music notes. It read: Humdroid.

Meredith tilted her head. "Did it come with those?" She pointed at one of the limbs.

Chantelle opened the slot as she answered. It swung down like an oven door. "We had to have them added as a special order. That's why we only have this one drone. It's expensive, you see." The assistant manager offered an apologetic smile. "We're hoping for something a little prettier if this project goes well. We'd like to have a slot in every guest room."

Meredith blinked theatrically. "Oh, my. That would be something. But I'm sorry, I didn't answer your question." She handed the drone her car keys while she spoke. It had a hand that appeared to be built specifically for keys. "I'll let the drone tell you how I feel," and she smiled coyly.

"What do you mean?" asked Chantelle.

Meredith only replied, "You'll see." Chantelle gasped as the hotel's drone returned carrying a version of itself that only had two basic forearms, and that could have fit snugly into a medium-sized suitcase.

Meredith smiled at Chantelle's hanging mouth. "I do apologize for not giving you warning," she said, presenting a business card with the Humdroid logo. "I didn't want your fine establishment up in arms about a personal visit."

Chantelle closed her mouth. Her expression was carefully blank.

"I'm not here for an inspection or anything," Meredith assured her, holding one hand palm-out. "The company's been getting a lot of orders here in Towerton, and I wanted to see for myself what the commotion was about."

Chantelle frowned. "But we arranged the entire project with the company and the town. Have you seen the local papers? A boy in town played a big part in it. No one's sure how old he is, but we think he's young. Calls himself Incendio."

"I've heard of some of those details, but I haven't actually read the paper. I'll look into that," she said with a professionally warmed smile. "And your arrangement with Humdroid was just one product. A hefty one, granted, but just one. I'm talking about the rest of the town. Just coming in, I could see them. From afar, Towerton looks like it's…got a flock of birds." She had to stop herself from comparing them to flies.

"Then why bring one of your own? I mean, if I might ask? Just curious," the assistant manager added.

After they took her car keys, her drone, and her suitcase and closed the wall slot, Meredith noticed that a handful of guests had come to see the hotel drone in use. "It pays to be prepared," she answered.

The assistant manager was already grabbing a flatbed cart to help her. "I suppose it does," the other woman replied, smiling at the onlookers.

They proceeded toward Meredith's room. The guests dispersed, though one of them went off with Chantelle because of concerns he had with his room. "End of the hall," Chantelle reminded Meredith. "Left side."

As she thanked the assistant manager and proceeded to her room, a little black girl followed her. She found her room and looked down at the girl. "Why, hello."

"My mommy's sad," said the girl.

"I'm sorry to hear that," Meredith replied, taken aback yet again. There was something at the back of her mind, or maybe the tip of her tongue, that was bothering her. *What am I so worried about?* "Where is she?"

Before the girl could respond, a dark man in a bright dress shirt rounded the corner at the end of the hall. "There you are," he said, looking at the girl. His strides were long, and he caught them up quickly.

"Is there pie?" the girl asked hopefully.

"Not yet, you little rascal, but soon," he answered and scooped her up in his arms. He smiled at Meredith, looking somewhere between playful and embarrassed. "Sorry, her brain is in her feet."

"Hey!" she gave the man her best indignant look.

Meredith laughed. "Not a problem."

They bid their farewells and Meredith entered her room, letting a sigh out of her nose. She was a professional now. Being around people shouldn't be awkward anymore. She shook her hair loose and set aside her baggage.

Two mornings later, Abigail Fischer left the roadside motel where she'd spent the night and sat atop the motorcycle Tasha had provided for her. That part was still a little surreal. Abby pulled out her phone. First, she texted Tasha:

I'm okay.

Tasha: The bed didn't kill you?

I was worried about the bike.

Tasha: I'm not. You'll be fine with that. Those motel beds, though...

Abby looked at her phone, and one corner of her lips quirked at that.

Thanks.

Tasha's response was an emoji of an upside-down smile. Not a frown; the head was upside-down. Shaking her head, Abby put the phone away and hit the highway for almost two hours before taking an off-ramp. She felt uncomfortable when the bike was still, when she was on streets, and when she was turning. But when she was on the highways, it was a little easier. Just go straight. Pick up speed. Don't do donuts.

She took a side road after the off-ramp and checked her phone's GPS to make sure she'd gone where she thought she had. There was a new message:

Chad: Near Towerton.

A flash of annoyance.

Thought I was doing this alone?

She waited a moment to see if there was an answer forthcoming. She was just about to put her phone away when she got one:

Chad: And you totally can. It's good to have back-up, though. Why don't we meet at the welcome mat, and take it from there?

I'm just scouting.

Chad: No one's talking about Jaycee. It's driving me nuts. Had to get out of the house, anyway. We'll just say hi, and I'll wait outside of town, if you want.

She didn't know what to say about Jaycee.

Alright. Right by the sign?

Chad: See you there!

It wasn't long before a green sign loomed: *Welcome to Towerton.*

Beneath it, leaning on a rental car, stood Chad. He waved when she drew near. She stopped and set one foot to the ground. Lifting the visor of her helmet, she said, "Hi."

"How's she treating you?" he asked, flicking a glance at the bike.

Abby shrugged. "I'm getting used to it."

"Didn't know you had a licence for motorbikes."

Abby was looking at the town. Chad frowned at her silence and turned around. "I know. Isn't it something?"

There were black dots in the air. It was hard to tell from here what they were. The town itself was standard enough: buildings, a gas station on the way, a water tower in the distance. "Did you race me here?" Abby asked.

"Huh? Oh, no." He put his hands in the pockets of his shorts. "I thought you'd be here first. Just didn't want to be too far behind."

"They're not moving like birds," Abby said suddenly.

Chad squinted. "You're right. Let's get a closer look."

"I'm just here to snoop around," she reminded him. "Victor said not to actually go into the town."

"Why did he ask you to go?" He'd stepped back a pace.

Abby watched him. "By myself? I don't know. He said he thinks I'm looking for something. Made some weird remark about Xeno."

"Yeah, he does that. Will we just take the car? Seems silly to use two vehicles just to look at the front door and turn around."

She looked around and shook her head. "You stay here, I'll drive around a bit and meet you back here."

He stood up straighter. "Are we cool?"

Abby looked at him like he was daft. "Yeah. We're cool. I'm just supposed to take a quick look around, and that's what I want to do. Something makes me nervous. I Googled the town in my motel room last night."

Chad absorbed all this and rubbed his chin. "…and?"

"Nothing. For months."

"Well, it is a small town."

"That's what I thought. Apparently, it literally started as a place people could go to get off the highway."

Chad laughed. "For real?"

Relieved by the turn away from tension, Abby chuckled a little too. Despite the fact that it was only spring, she was not liking the heat now that there was no highway wind. "Yeah, it's just far enough from everything that it fits kinda snug in the middle of nowhere. They deal in supplies. Rope and camping stuff, car repairs, basic things you need on the road. You know."

Chad nodded. "Doesn't sound like Victor's usual thing. All right, let's get this over with."

"See you in a bit!" Abby said, and started off. As she approached the town, she started feeling a little anxious. She shook her head. She watched the dots grow and looked for a turn so she could go around the outskirts of the town. Then two things registered to her: those dots in the air were machines, and Chad was driving behind her. She pulled over.

Chad went past her, followed suit, and walked back.

"What's up?" he said.

"Why are you following me?"

Chad ran a hand through his hair. "Call it a hunch. Don't you feel a little worried?"

"No," she lied. She lifted her chin and flicked her gaze behind him.

Turning, Chad had to acknowledge she was right. "That must be a few dozen drones."

"At least."

"Hard to tell with all the moving about," he remarked. Then he looked around. It was a slow, almost three-sixty-degree turn.

"What?" Abby asked.

"You see any traffic?"

"Nope."

"In any direction?"

"Should I?" Abby replied. "I mean, it's a small town.

Even their advertising practically says, 'Great to see you, please keep moving.'"

Chad laughed. "Yeah. I dunno. Gut feeling, I guess. Let's just drive straight through the town, then we can turn around and go right back."

"But-"

"You got a rabbit's foot in there?" He nodded at the bags behind the bike's seat.

Abby hesitated. "Well, it would be faster…"

"That's the spirit!"

Thatcher, meanwhile, was taking a break from gaming. At the moment, he was frowning at his screen. The tattered remains of a TV dinner lay on the nearest surface he could find: a bookshelf. He'd clean up when he next stepped away from his computer.

He was reading e-mails that included the mayor of the town, local news and communication networks, and several local businesses. Thatcher had never seen circumlocution like the mayor's. Their project with the drones was going well. Apparently, the town even had a visitor from Humdroid.

There was pressure to go public about their progress.

The argument went as follows: get the press in on the events, and there would be investors and other financial backing on the horizon. But get them in too soon, and the town risked looking foolish. The mayor, in essence, wanted a fully successful project before they unveiled it. The appearance of this Humdroid employee, whose role wasn't actually stated, was making both sides of the argument push harder — and therefore listen less.

But the media, according to one of the reporters who

was part of the discussion, had already gotten word of the state funding that was going into supplying the municipal service drones. Just a few days ago, Thatcher's proposed unit of experimental service drones had arrived.

"Los Reparadors to the Rescue!" read the headline on the local paper. Thatcher, of course, read the article on-line. There was a picture of two flying drones handling a garbage bin at the end of someone's driveway. The photo included some of the frame of the window from which it had been taken. When he asked about it by e-mail, Thatcher was told it was supposed to "convey a home-of-the-everyman vibe."

He thought it looked unprofessional.

Pushing back, he spun his chair by pressing against the horizontal bar of the legs with his feet. Spinning back and forth, he mulled over his position. Behind him was a degree he'd hung from the wall. MIT. Computer Science and Course 15-1: Management. He kept it there not as a reminder of the achievement, but as a reminder of the fact that he'd barely passed.

He turned back to his three screens. The centre one displayed his e-mail conversation. Flanking that screen were two screens of porn. Thatcher felt that business and politics were smutty undertakings, despite the fact that he excelled at business. Cracking his fingers, he went to work composing his response:

Esteemed Colleagues,

I agree that we should have a short delay before press releases and public announcements. Towerton should be well-represented when the project bears its fruit. Yet at the end of the day, this is an investment, so we should not delay too long. I recommend that we bring together the entire town for this initiative. Already I've noticed independent agents ordering their drones from suppliers other than the business I began two months ago. The hotel and the hospital, among others, are also running their own initiatives.

Bringing everyone together for this will take time, but I look forward to seeing what our townspeople can do. I must express gratitude for the support many of you have shown, financially and otherwise, in getting my small business up and running. Humdroid has surpassed my sales in dollars but not units sold, because mine are smaller and more accessibly priced. Perhaps we might convene with them? Please advise.

With respect,

Incendio

He clicked Send, then grabbed a portable (but still rather large) control console and set it up at his desk, connecting it to his computer. Two of the cameras were his own additions, and he didn't like the display on the control unit itself. So, he had created software that automatically linked his computer to all three cameras whenever he attached the controls to it. In the left screen was the feed from the camera beneath his drone. In the centre was the front camera. His right screen displayed the view from behind the drone.

He put on a headset that included a microphone and guided his drone into the air.

Abby and Chad pulled into the first parking lot they could find. It belonged to a mom-and-pop diner. So eager were they to get away from their vehicles that they parked at oblong angles, terribly mismatched from the parking spots. Abby tore her helmet off and dropped it in her eagerness to secure it to her bike.

She left it there.

The pair ran to the diner and found it locked and closed.

"Why are they closed!?" demanded Chad through heavy breathing.

Abby gasped a few times, swallowed, and shook her head. They were sweating, and both told themselves it was the sun beating down on them. It wasn't yet noon.

They stayed next to the wall of the building, getting as much shade as they could, and walked around the corner so that they were facing the street; the door had been on the side. Backs to the window, breath restored, they watched as three drones floated down in front of them. They were all equipped with speakers.

A fourth drone came in sidelong. "Hey, it's Incendio!" said a man through the speaker.

Thatcher turned his drone in response, so that he could see the one that was speaking. He recognized the voice. From his drone came his rough voice. Chad thought it sounded too young to be as grizzled and grumbly as it was. "Hi, Shore. Did you bring the newcomer?"

"Nope," came from the first speaker. Then it sounded like a little girl. "Daddy, can I play with the throne?"

"It's a drone, sweetie. And no," said the man's voice. "This is grown-up stuff."

"You never let me play with your toys."

"It's not a toy!"

A woman's voice came from Shore's speaker, though

distantly. "Alex…"

"Pew pew!" said the girl's voice.

"Okay, later," said the original voice. "We have company."

Chad and Abby looked at each other. All three of the other drones were facing Shore's. Abby coughed. "…do you guys live here?"

"Yep!" answered Shore.

"I do not," replied one of the larger ones. It could still squeeze into a suitcase, Abby thought. "I'm Meredith. Pleased to meet you all."

There was a chorus of greeting. "I'm Chad," he chimed in to get things rolling, "and this is Abby." He pointed at the one calling itself Shore. "Are you Shore, or Alex, or a bunch of people?"

The little girl laughed. A second voice, apparently a different girl, said, "Mom, we're out of cookies." Abby giggled despite herself. Chad looked at her and grinned awkwardly. Abby's face was tight.

"I'm Shore."

"He's Alex," said the background woman.

"That's my wife. She's trouble. Oof!" There was a whumping sound. The girls giggled.

"Can any of you get that hair off my camera?" said the only drone that hadn't spoken yet. "It's driving me nuts."

Abby stepped forward. Chad looked up and down the street. No one. His rental and Abby's bike looked ridiculous, but they were the only ones on the lot. Abby frowned. "It's not a hair. It's a crack."

On the other end of that drone sat a young petite Hispanic woman. Her control scheme was not as large and sophisticated as Thatcher's, and her computer sat off to the side. On the screen for her controls, the crack occupied just enough space to draw attention.

She cursed.

"That's Crumb," Thatcher's drone said for him.

"So you all have gamertags?" said Meredith's drone.

"Yeah, pretty much," Thatcher answered as Incendio.

"I'll be…uh…Chap Stick!" came Meredith's voice.

"Look out, we're in for some Chap!" said Shore.

"You're the worst," remarked Crumb.

"We'll see about that," replied Shore. "We should keep…droning on and on!"

Meredith groaned.

Thatcher could not position his drone to keep everyone in view at once. He turned decidedly away from Shore. Abby giggled tightly. Thatcher was having a hard time looking at the newcomers. They were strangers. He tugged on one ear. There was a knot in his stomach. He wanted to have his drone leave. Or get them to leave.

"Anywhere indoors we can take this?" Chad asked. His fingers twitched.

"I'm at the hotel, if that helps," Meredith ventured. "Do you two happen to have any drones?"

"Uh, no," Abby stammered. "We're…just passing through."

Meredith adjusted her bathrobe. She'd only meant to go on a test spin, but these were the only two people she'd seen on the streets besides herself since she arrived a couple of days ago. There wasn't even any litter populating the streets. She absently applied her chap stick.

Abby's heart sank at the prospect of going all the way to the hotel. It was down the road. Six or seven minutes' slow walk. Chad licked his lips. "We — I — well, it's just, the heat. Yeah. It's different than out west. There's wind when we need it."

"Why don't we let you folks find more comfortable arrangements?" Thatcher suggested diplomatically.

"If I could," Meredith interjected, "I'd really like to have a word with those of you using drones. Do you have a club, or a place to meet?"

"We have clubs in spades!" Shore said.

"Please stop," said Crumb.

"Aced it!" Shore retorted with a chuckle. There was another whump, and his wife's voice distantly came through with, "Be good, dear."

"Yeah," Abby said, louder than she meant to, "let's be on our way."

"N-nice meeting you!" Chad said and waved as the machines all bade their farewells and flew away together. He was running almost the moment they turned away.

Abby watched only long enough to notice that "Incendio" was flying far more skillfully than the other three pilots. He had more cameras, too. Then she ran after Chad. She was still in her biking gear, and sweating bullets, but couldn't stop to take them off.

They tried two doors before barrelling into a house. As soon as they were in, Abby took off her chaps and her jacket, recklessly tossing her red hair about as though struggling with a spider web. Chad stood farther in, hands on knees, catching his breath.

"Hello," said a Hispanic man.

They both jumped.

"It's all right," he said placidly. "I won't hurt you."

The pair looked at each other. Abby awkwardly gathered up her things. The man leaned against the wall of the hallway, entirely at ease. He had lithe musculature. His eyes were chocolate brown and sharp as nails.

He wore jeans and a Slipknot T-shirt.

"Who…?" started Chad.

"Please, set that down there," the man said, pointing to a two-level bookshelf at the beginning of the hallway. Since she had nothing better to do, Abby obliged. As she and Chad stepped through the doorway out of the porch, the stranger stood properly and turned around. "Join me," he spoke without looking back at them. "I was just brewing tea."

They found themselves in a kitchen/dining room combo. Three piping mugs soon adorned the table. The door to the back yard — little more than a patch of grass between two fences — was just past the table.

Abby sat and started drinking the tea without a word, watching the man curiously. Chad stood with his hands on the back of a chair. The stranger sat and sipped. Chad looked between the two in bewilderment, then turned his attention to the stranger. "You're not in any of the pictures I've seen in the house. And all the people in the pictures are white."

Abby sputtered.

"That's because this isn't my house," the man replied amicably.

Abby put down her mug. "Okay, what's going on here?"

She kept darting uncomfortable glances at Chad. Steam wafted past him, tea untouched, as he sat and levelled his best glare at the stranger.

"My name is Geronimo," said the Hispanic as he took another sip of tea. His calm gaze centred upon Abby.

She absently tossed some of her red hair with her left hand. Her right gripped the handle of the mug. "Why are you here if this isn't your house?"

Gripping his mug with both hands, Geronimo sighed. "Step outside," he said, nodding to the door that was barely four feet from Abby.

"You're being weird," Chad pointed out. "Why should we do anything you say?"

"Just do it," Geronimo replied, looking Chad in the eye.

"Look, clearly something is wrong with this town," Abby joined in before Chad could test his luck. "Why won't you just fill us in?"

"Step outside."

Abby stood suddenly and headed for the door. "Ah, hey," Chad interjected, turning his head but keeping his eyes on Geronimo. "Don't."

She looked out the window. "It's not a big yard."

"Step outside."

"We're gonna leave soon," Chad said, "but you should at least tell us why you're in this house. Did you hurt—"

"Step outside."

Abby inspected the door, looking through its window every which way. "No sign of anything off," she remarked.

"Step outside."

"Dammit," Chad started, but Abby put her hand on the knob.

Silence.

"This is rubbish," Abby said, taking her hand off the knob. "Just answer wo-"

"Step. Out. Side."

Abby looked out the window.

Chad stood and walked around the table on her side, either to be closer to Abby or farther from Geronimo. He opened his mouth, half-lifting a hand toward her, but said nothing as she moved.

As the Hispanic lifted his mug to his lips again, the redhead took a deep breath. She took another. Sweat sheened her brow. Swiftly, she yanked the door open and stood upon the back step of the house. The door could not close behind her before she bolted back in.

"Care to try?" After three heartbeats, Chad realized Geronimo was talking to him. He stared at the door. He wiped his lips.

His tea was untouched.

Glancing at Abby, he turned to face Geronimo head-on. "We're done here. Play your games with someone else."

With that, Chad marched out of the room. He heard footsteps behind him. Turning left in the hallway, he entered the living room with the intention of looking out the large window there.

Geronimo leaned against the entryway, arms folded, and said, "Card fan?"

Chad was surprised by a thin surge of hope and kept his expression flat.

"Care for some poker? I have an open pack in the other room."

"We're not settling in," Abby cut in. She looked at Chad.

He stayed silent. She shifted and sweat made her clothes feel more ragged than they really were. Swallowing, she marched to the window to study the unpeopled world outside.

"I've been here three weeks," Geronimo said suddenly.

The pair faced him.

"Awful lot of drones in the air," Abby remarked.

"What's going on in this town?" Chad finally asked.

"I'm not sure," Geronimo sighed.

Abby repeated her earlier sentiment: "We can't stay."

"You can't leave," answered Geronimo a little too quickly. An edge in his tone recalled fear, but Abby couldn't tell if it was to threaten or implore.

Chad took out his phone and started typing.

Geronimo started, "Who are y—"

"Never mind," said Abby. Then: "We should leave as a group."

Geronimo and Chad looked at each other and then the woman. "I thought we didn't trust him?" Chad pointed out as he returned his phone to his pocket. His text to Victor had been simple: Something's wrong not sure what with Abby can't leave.

"If we stick together," Abby reasoned, "we might be able to work through whatever's making us want to stay inside."

Geronimo shook his head. "I can't be seen."

The pair looked at each other. Chad voiced the obvious suspicion: "What happened to the people who lived here?"

Geronimo blinked, then laughed. "The place was empty. Didn't you see my car on the lawn?"

Abby returned to the window. The grass was torn in two swathes of the tires' violence. "I guess we were in such a rush to get in…"

"Well, you weren't the only ones," Geronimo pointed out.

There was a pause. Chad took a deep breath. "Three weeks, huh?"

Geronimo looked away, but then nodded.

Abby marched out of the room, Chad in tow.

Geronimo was slow to follow and spoke as they were putting on shoes. Abby looked at her road gear and wished she'd thought to take it off as soon as she'd gotten off the bike. But the panic…

Geronimo stood squarely in the hallway. "Where are you going?"

They had their shoes on. Abby's chaps and jacket were still on the bookshelf. The pair looked at each other. "Not sure," Chad replied.

"We have to keep moving," Abby added. Suddenly, she picked up her road gear and held it out to the Hispanic. "Gerry," she said, ignoring his twitch at the name, "there's a motorcycle next to a car at the diner's parking lot. We did the same parking job you did." She felt a flush of self-consciousness, but soldiered on: "Please leave my stuff with that bike. I'd like to be able to leave in a hurry, and I'm too warm with them on."

"I can't leave," he said flatly.

"We have to fight this," she said. "Keep your head down and just do it. Don't look around. No one's watching."

Chad watched as the man stepped forward and slowly retrieved her gear. Neither of the two noticed his wonder.

Abby had her phone out. "Give me your number."

Geronimo frowned.

"Just do it," Chad said. "She stepped out the back to make your point. It's your turn."

They exchanged numbers.

Abby called him, right in front of him. The Hispanic looked at his phone. "Is this some white girl game?"

She held his gaze, her phone at her ear. "Just keep talking to me, focus on getting my stuff to the bike, then come straight back here. That's all you have to do."

"I don't have to—"

She ripped open the front door, forced a nonplussed Chad through, and marched them both to the right. Over her shoulder and into her phone, she barked at Geronimo. "Out the door, head down, move, move, move!"

Chad looked back at her in astonishment, but she pushed hard at his shoulder with her free hand, facing him forward again. As soon as Geronimo was out the door, he tried to turn back, but she rushed back and pulled it closed, shouldering at the muscled man. She didn't have the brawn to much affect him, but she just kept ordering: "Move! Gear to bike! Move!"

She jabbed a finger for Chad's benefit. "We're going to the hotel!"

"Why-" Chad started.

"We just are." It was almost totally windless, and her hair felt like spider webs.

"I could grab my car," huffed Geronimo.

"No!"

"I'm clo—"

"Bike! Gear! Move!" She turned as she ran. "I said NO! Not the car! Run to the diner! GO!"

Tears stung Chad's eyes. He forced them on the hotel down the road. A doorway went by.

The houses registered less than the doors. Once, Abby started to veer to one of them. He pulled her back on course. But she did the same for him twice. Somewhere nearby, dogs were barking. Then he was inside and felt hollow. It took him a moment to realize that it was the emotional echo of having slammed the door behind him. It opened again almost immediately.

Abby demanded, "What are you doing? We need to kee—"

Even as they were breathing hard, they had to plug their noses. With the blood rushing in their ears, the buzzing was also slow to get through to them. They glanced at each other as they stepped past the living room. There were pictures, books, and figurines with a pirate theme, as well as some posters, maps, and travel books. "We need to…" and she walked, hypnotically, towards the buzzing.

She knew she should get out of the house. She knew there was nothing those flies could show her that she'd want to see. She pictured herself returning to the front door. Bullets smashing through it, feet and black clothes and shouting. Something erased. Fire and guilt.

Stars were gathering in her eyes before she realized she was holding her breath. She was at a threshold. One hand pinched her nose and covered her mouth so she could keep out the thickening cloud.

She felt sick, but she had to know. Steeling herself, she hastily stepped into the doorway.

A body hung from the ceiling of a walk-in closet. Mercifully, she couldn't get a good look with all the flies about. Back in the living room she found Chad listening to the answering machine.

"…we're sorry about the inconvenience, but please stop calling about the barking. We're a dog pound. Consider finding a more suitable…"

She tuned it out as she headed for the front door.

"Geronimo?" she said thickly to the phone shaking in her hand. He'd hung up. When had that happened?

Chad was the white of ice as they reached the door.

Her hand was on the knob.

"I don't have his number," Chad muttered.

"I can't…" her voice cracked. It was just a door. The sunlight was lovely. No wind and a stray cloud or two. In the distance, barking.

"Close your eyes," Chad said.

"What?"

"Look, I don't know how you got us this far, but I think you were on to something about working together. Turn the knob, Abby."

Her breathing was heavy because she was standing in front of an open door with her eyes closed.

"Follow the wall," she said. "We'll both have to keep

our eyes closed."

He hadn't realized he's stepped backward. His heart fired a hard pulse of embarrassment.

Bordering on hyperventilation, she clung to the wall with most of her right side, pushing the door as far back as it would go while she slowly wormed her way over the threshold. All the while they talked: "Did you get Geronimo's number too?"

He kept moving. She heard him fumble for his phone. "No, but I'm getting messages."

They made it to the corner of the house. Ahead was a T-section. From somewhere to her right, she could hear jingling metal, accented by panting or the sound of lapping water. "I think I found the dog pound. This town is really quiet."

"Except the drones."

"Yeah," she said. "Are you okay?"

"I...I can't do this."

"Yes, you can. What were the messages?"

"I can't right now. I need to focus on..." He fidgeted behind her.

"...whatever's keeping people indoors," she finished for him.

Abby had her face pressed against the siding of the house. She was hugging the corner with her eyes closed. "All right," she said, "I'm gonna cross the str-..." she swallowed. "...the street." Taking two deep breaths, she opened her eyes and ran for all she was worth. Chad was beside her. They did their best not to look at the houses. Her eyes were on the sidewalk.

When she looked up to get her bearings, a lovely blue

door caught her eye. She was through it before she even realized what she was doing.

"Abby? ABBY!?" burst through her focus. It was coming from Chad, outside.

There was a soft, feminine sound from the stairwell around the corner from the porch where she stood. It was like a high-pitched groan, almost a whine. "I...um..." she said to while she walked the five or six feet it took to investigate.

"Come back!" Chad said. "We can't stay inside!" He had his eyes closed, body pressed against the wall, fighting the urge to go in.

"Oh my god..." Abby whispered as she turned to find an old woman crumpled at the bottom of the stairs. She looked like a poorly bagged bundle of broken sticks. The woman looked up at her and suddenly all pain melted from the senior's expression. There is a glint in a person's eye when they are ready to sleep, and ready to say goodbye. Like starlight on black water, it shifted just once as the elderly woman noticed the young one.

Then it was still.

Abby raised her hand to her mouth at the heartbreaking sight, only to notice the air in front of her rippling with rapidly growing waves of heat.

Chad felt it. "Abby?"

Something was wrong.

Thatcher paced his basement, running the fingers of both hands through his head of hefty but clean hair. He hated the stereotype of the unwashed nerd. His fingernails were meticulously filed and his hair well-brushed. Almost giddy with nervous energy, he'd cleared away the garbage in the basement, vacuumed and dusted, and was now struggling with what to do. He'd tried a dozen games to distract himself, including the MMO Eve Online and some roleplay chat rooms, but the situation was irking him. A file for an e-book in the niche genre of litRPG sat open but unread on the left screen of his computer setup.

The right screen showed Instagram. He'd phished to get access to a townsperson's account so as to remove their post about all the drone activity, then changed their password so they wouldn't be able to do it again. Something was wrong in this town, and he needed all his ducks in a row to deal with it. How had he come to be responsible for so much? It was like people were only driven when he was, and they withdrew when he did.

But that was ridiculous.

The centre screen now showed a message from Kagami, an albino Japanophile he knew from his circle of drone friends. Her message said that a redhead and a blond had been seen running from a house that was now on fire, according to a friend who'd messaged her. Still no answer from Crossbones, the cynophobic fan of pirates.

He'd started pacing after a surge of problems: a fight had broken out in the hospital. Someone barred the mental health ward in an act of cowardice that he thought was barbaric. People were panicking. The hospital's Internet went down, and no one was sure why. A massive rat problem had cropped up around the grocery store because it had been unattended for so long.

Thatcher was furious. What was everyone hiding from?

He marched over to the ground-level window and

peeked out through the curtain. No more rock doves. Upstairs, he went to the guest room, where he kept his drone. Daylight cast a slightly blue hue through the closed curtain. Now that he was finished with maintenance and battery charging, he brought it out to the front door and set it down in the porch. The blinds on the door were closed. Returning to the basement, he began his flight routine, changing all the screens of the computer display to the drone's cameras.

He was proud of how skilled he'd become. He was able to make it lift off, open the door, and close the door behind it.

Geronimo was finding it harder to stay outside with every door he passed. He rounded a corner, considering jumping more fences. He was back on the street he started and realized that the hotel was far in front of him. Beyond that would be the place where he'd been staying.

"Who the devil are you!? Get off my lawn!" someone shouted at him.

A drone, sidelong to Geronimo, flew out of a house on a side street. Smoke was rising from a couple of blocks away. He was running, trying to get away from a cloud of drones that kept bombarding him with questions. He was wearing a ski mask he kept in his pocket in case he needed to quickly cover his face. They couldn't know who he was. That was critical.

Chad and Abby, meanwhile, ran at the hotel. It had floor-to-ceiling windows. People inside were staring. They made a mad dash for the front door.

Thatcher guided his drone toward the pillar of smoke and rose higher to try for a better view. *What was taking the fire department?* He cursed the warm, dry weather. The fire had spread. Messages started popping up on his screen. He couldn't keep up with most of them. One was disturbing:

Shore: Crumb's drone just dropped out of the air!

He noticed then that there were several rooftops with drones on them. Doing nothing. One was near solar panels. Was it charging? There could have been any number of reasons. But with so many drones in the air, he shouldn't have been that surprised — what goes up and all that. At least two houses near the fire had caught. Was Crumb in one of them?

He flew to the closest house, where he saw someone in the living room window. What was that glitter? As he approached, the figure disappeared. Nearing the front door, he was shocked when it whipped open and projectiles began bouncing off of his precious drone. The man in the door was wearing — Thatcher couldn't believe it — a tin foil hat.

An actual, straight-up, tin foil hat.

The man was shouting: "I KNEW YOU'D COME! But no alien's takin' Ashton James!"

"Stop it! I'm not—"

"I know you're putting that fear in me! Well, I'M NOT AFRAID OF YOU!"

Thatcher didn't bother pointing out the contradiction. "Your house is on fi—"

"Yeah! Tryin' ta smoke me out! IT WON'T WORK! Ain't no alien probing me!"

"Listen! Stop!" But even as he shouted, Thatcher had to withdraw. There was too much going on. Even as he backed it out and away, his fingers flew over the keyboard.

He was looking for the town fire department, trying to get in contact with the hospital or an ambulance service, reaching out to his drone friends, and flying his own drone in search of the newcomers who've been making ripples in the grapevine since that morning. Then he remembered: there was a woman from Humdroid. Was this about competition with a drone company? Would they do that?

He turned his drone toward the hotel.

Abby was in the lobby. Meredith entered from a hallway, wondering what all the commotion was about.

"Lady," said one of the tenants, "you're loco. We don't have to go on a field trip with you!"

"I'm not saying all of you need to leave! Just one of you! Anyone!" Abby had both hands in front of her, pleading with a small gathering. Chad stood closer to the door, struggling to come up with a better game plan than simply getting people out of doors until things make sense.

The clerk had stepped out from the counter and was busily sweeping the area and washing surfaces. He checked his mask obsessively and tried to only be around people when he was behind them.

The black man Meredith met in the corridor when she arrived stepped forward. "Young lady," he said, "I think perhaps you're having some trouble with the sun…"

"Stop calling me lady!"

Meredith wended her way through the group. "Excuse me," she said with well-honed business tact, "but may I ask what it is you're looking for?"

"I need help," Abby replied.

"Obviously," someone snarked beneath her breath. Abby ignored the other woman.

"I just docked my drone to charge," Meredith said. "I noticed a fire…"

Abby's lip quivered. She shook her head. "That's gonna have to be for the fire department," she replied.

Before she could continue, a passing maid said, "They won't come. Bunch of lazy good-for-nothings at town hall…"

There was general assent. "People here are weird," said a young Hispanic boy. He was holding the hand of the man who'd called Abby "loco."

"I'm just waiting to get my affairs in order," said a middle-aged woman who was checking her cell phone compulsively. "Then I'm out of here."

"Yeah," said a teenaged girl. "If I could breathe a little better, I'd be gone too."

"But you got the air tank you said you were waiting for," pointed out the black man's daughter.

Incensed, the teenager folded her arms. The oxygen tank was in her bookbag, and tubes led from there to her nose. "I can't drive with that thing hooked up to me. I'm waiting for my family."

Meredith stepped closer to Abby as the rest of the group began getting into similar stories and questioning each other. "I need more cleaning supplies!" the clerk called out to the same maid, who was now headed in the other direction.

"What kind of help did you need?" she asked, leaning forward to be heard over the rising din. Snippets got in: something about insects. Another person didn't trust the chemicals in the air outside, complaining that the highway should be patrolled for trucks with questionable products.

Abby opened her mouth, unsure of how to respond. A woman started crying, saying there were predators and that she couldn't leave "while the police were lazing about."

Someone kicked over a chair and started shouting. Abby grabbed Meredith and pulled her to the door. "Something's wrong," she said simply.

"Yes, I got that," Meredith said, "but please don't yank on me. Stop. No, wait!"

But Abby nearly dragged her to the door. "Step outside."

Chad put a hand on Abby's arm. She locked eyes with him and realized that she was feeling the same distress. She released the other woman.

Meredith took in the lovely sunny day. A butterfly flew past the windows. Drones danced distantly in the sky. "What's this about?" Meredith objected.

"We're not sure yet," Chad said.

Abby added, "Just step outside."

"We should get this—" Meredith started, turning toward the frothing of the crowd.

"We need to go," Abby cut her off.

Meredith looked at the door — and through it — with frustration. She glanced at Chad, Abby, and the crowd behind her. "Some of these people have been here for weeks..."

"You're new here?" Abby asked.

The Humdroid employee nodded.

"That explains why you seem more level-headed…" Chad mused aloud.

"I'm a professional," Meredith bristled. When neither moved, a fog of doubt descended upon her. And there was a sense of urgency she couldn't explain, like she had a thousand things to look into and no one to help her. She ran a hand through her hair. "I'm not really staying to make a better business case for when I leave, am I?"

"Probably not," Abby agreed. Then: "Hold my hand."

People started throwing punches. A hollow and muffled metallic *ding* rang out as the girl with the oxygen tank hit the floor. Chad watched the crowd with mounting horror. Meredith blinked at the redhead, but she slowly complied. Then Abby locked elbows with Chad.

The crowd was getting out of hand. Two children were crying. Someone was screaming. The clerk was shouting for them to stop.

Meredith and Abby stood by the door, a window set in a wall of windows. Some pigeons landed on the ground to the left of the door and congregated with a calm that Abby couldn't understand. Couldn't they see the fighting? Why weren't they concerned?

"Look at me," Abby said.

"This is crazy," said Meredith.

Abby nodded. She and Chad began barrelling them all through the door. "No one stays behind," Chad said.

Every time one of them was about to give up and turn back inside, the others pushed forward.

On the fourth attempt, they got out of the hotel.

Thatcher was torn. He'd just caught sight of the entangled trio as they half-shambled, half-ran in the middle of the road. They looked ridiculous. He followed them as they went right from the door, eventually turning right again — onto his street. He couldn't tell what they were thinking.

As the trio made that turn, Chad looked up and huffed, "Is that Gerry?" The mask didn't hide the outfit, the build, or the style of movement.

Thatcher mostly just saw the cloud of drones. They seemed to be harassing someone, but they were too far away for him to identify. He cursed the drone cameras; if their resolution were a little better…

He spun the drone around to see if there were anything else in the area, just in time to see another one. "Look out!" he shouted uselessly as there was a collision. His screens turned to snow.

In unison, the trio wailed in dismay and tumbled all over each other. "What was that!?" Chad sputtered as he and the others picked themselves up.

Abby said, "You felt it too?" And immediately felt stupid; they'd all wailed.

Meredith watched this "Gerry" use his size twelve skeleton key to enter two doors down. Without thinking, she yanked the others once and simply ran after him.

As soon as they were inside, Chad savaged his way down the second set of stairs to the left. The first went up. The front door was broken behind them, and something primal made the lower levels radiate safety. Abby clung to the closest thing she could find. It was the rail. Gerry was in the kitchen ahead of them, turning and looking back at them with heaving lungs. Meredith was sprawled out on the floor. Everyone had a flood of emotions that included terror and…

"Are you…does that…?" Meredith struggled to pull herself up from the floor and the panic.

"It's like…" Abby wiped her eyes and nose "…like, I dunno, puberty or something. It's all coming at me at once."

Meredith was nodding as they both heard Thatcher. He was standing in the centre of his basement room, regarding Chad with outrage. "Who are you, and why are you in my house?"

Chad's hands were up, palm out. "Listen," he started.

The two women stepped down to the half-landing, so that they had to crouch to see Thatcher over Chad's shoulder. The three intruders were visibly trembling. Thatcher's eyes were glassy with suspicion and fear.

"I know you!" The Hispanic's voice was higher in pitch because of his mounting panic. His breaths came shallow and quick, and sweat beaded his forehead. "Chad and Abby!" He pointed at them frantically.

"Incendio," Chad's eyes widened as he spoke. "Why are…how did…" The card aficionado was looking at the three-screen setup behind Thatcher with a kind of awe. There was nothing but snow, but still: what had the Hispanic been up to?

"You're not how I pictured you from your voice," Abby remarked. Chad turned, and both he and Meredith regarded Abby with incredulity. "…what?" She asked. Her speech, like Chad's, was tight and strained.

"I get that a lot," the pilot of Incendio replied dryly.

"Now, what the hell are you doing in my house?" With Herculean effort, he was suppressing his terror with glib humour.

Someone's phone was vibrating.

"Aren't you going to get that?" asked Meredith.

Thatcher noticed that these three seemed to be calming the more that he worked down his fear, controlled his breathing, and strove to come across to them as poised. In fact, they seemed to be mirroring him. But that was ludicrous. He was just thrown off by their presence.

The Hispanic gauged the three intruders. They did not seem eager to hurt him. His nervousness jangled with every vibration of Chad's phone. Abby and Meredith both shivered the way that Thatcher wanted to.

"Are you the one doing this to Towerton?" Abby asked. Meredith merely watched the Hispanic. Chad furrowed his brow.

"Doing what?" Thatcher asked. He mused about how he might fight the three of them off. The Internet was his best and most comfortable weapon, but it didn't use bullets.

"You're not gonna tell me you didn't know something's not right?" Chad scoffed.

Thatcher regarded the intruder with open hostility. "Yeah. Like, why are you in my house?"

The three looked at each other, suddenly abashed.

Thatcher pressed his advantage: "Get out and I'll give you a head start before calling the cops."

"Okay, okay, let's not get ahead of ourselves…" Meredith chimed in.

"Maybe we should all sit down?" Abby offered.

Thatcher frowned. "This is my house. What are you gringos doing?"

"Hey!" Chad stood up a little straighter.

"Get," Thatcher punctuated, looking the other man in the eye, "Out."

"Please," Abby said. It came out with Thatcher's hostility, which confused her.

Chad decided to take a gamble: "Look, we came here because something's wrong. It's been noticed. And now that we're here—"

"I don't care," Thatcher interrupted. "For the last time," and his voice rose, "Get! Out!"

They all felt a ballooning mixture of anger, fear, pride, and outrage. But there was also an awkward, embarrassed flush. Chad stepped forward to speak, and then there were footsteps upstairs. "Hello?" called Geronimo's voice.

Unaccountably, everyone in the room had a cold shock run from heartbeat to rising hair.

Thatcher frowned and looked up at the stairs behind the trio, muttering, "Geronimo?"

The well-muscled Hispanic man appeared at the top of the stairs just as the trio began talking at once. Everyone turned to face him.

"Who are you?" asked Meredith.

Then there was an impossible flare of rage. Everyone's knuckles went bone white with it, though four of the people there didn't know where it was coming from.

Thatcher roared, "WHAT ARE YOU DOING HERE!?"

"So, it's true!" Geronimo declared as he bulled his way down the stairs. The women had to flatten against the wall to get out of the way, and Chad stepped aside.

"GET OUT!" Thatcher roared. He looked around, weaponless.

To everyone's surprise, Chad stepped forward and slugged Geronimo in the face. He nursed his hand as his target, barely phased, stared at him in surprise.

The muscular man said, "What was that?"

"I...I don't know," replied a throbbing and baffled Chad.

Every heart in the room pulsed with confusion and electric anger.

"Why is everyone treating my house like Town Hall?" Thatcher demanded. "And how dare you?" He was looking at Geronimo.

The well-muscled Hispanic regarded the pudgy, pale Hispanic with a closed fist, a tense jaw, and eyes that shone with sadness. "I have some explaining to do..."

Thatcher barked a mirthless laugh. "Finally catching on, huh?"

"You never would call me Dad..." the man sighed.

Thatcher flared. "A foster father isn't a father!"

"I suppose I should introduce myself," Geronimo replied. "My name is..." he managed slowly.

"Geronimo," Thatcher interrupted. "Yes, yes, now tell m—"

"...Soto," the man continued. Abby and Chad had a moment of small, static emotional shock. Then it was as though everyone's skulls were suffused with thunder and blood. "Soto Verra," he finished with obvious gravity, turning back to Thatcher.

The younger Hispanic never said a word, but the other three exploded in rage. "Why did you lie to us!?" Abby demanded. Tears burned their way down her cheeks. Yet here she was, in Thatcher's house, an intruder furious at an intrusion.

Meredith was silent. Her expression shifted as she looked at each person who spoke. Everything had gravity, as if the situation were hers personally. But she didn't know these people. There was no context for the anger, resentment, shock, and so on. What was going on?

Chad was experiencing a different transportation of wrath. He stood stock still and stared at Soto as though seeing into or through the other man. Everyone was white-knuckled.

Thatcher cursed. Once. In Spanish. Everything grew still. There was a crashing sound in the distance. People were shouting, but it was so faint as only to be heard in quiet.

"I had to protect you," Soto said.

Everyone felt sick inside. Chad remained a colossus of stillness.

Thatcher, too, stared at the older Hispanic. "That's your play? You weren't keeping me in a bubble, Gerry."

"Son, please—"

"I am not your son!"

Soto held out an ID card. Thatcher wasn't interested, but Chad could see it from where he was standing. Soto Verra, Shane Industries.

"What's going on here?" Meredith said.

Soto sighed. He turned to the trio. "I'm his father."

"Bullshit!" Thatcher erupted. "You fostered me when I was almost old enough to move out!"

"I chased you in the system for years."

"Chad?" Abby stepped forward and laid a hand on his shoulder. He didn't respond.

Soto searched Chad's eyes. He looked at the women. "Please, let us have a moment of privacy."

"No," Thatcher said sharply. Suddenly, the strangers were less frightening than just being alone with...Soto. "Enough is enough. I'm a grown man now, and I'll have answers."

"Seems we're all kinda lost," Meredith remarked.

There was another brief silence, punctuated by distant shouts, crashing sounds, the shattering of a door, and screams.

"I really am—" Soto started.

Thatcher's interruption was harsh and sudden. "You there. What are you staring at?" Abby had to shake Chad's shoulder before he blinked, frowned, and looked at her. "Answer me!" pressed their host.

Chad looked between Thatcher and Abby, then sheepishly watched his shoes. "I'm...I'm not sure. I mean, I wanted bad luck for...uh...Soto, but..." and he ineffectually rolled his hands a few times as if to wring words from the air.

Soto was shocked. "Whatever for?"

"We're all angry at you," Abby said, looking around at everyone. "I think you're even angry at yourself." Her voice hushed and took on a hollow tone: "...but I don't know where that's coming from."

Chad's mouth worked, but he didn't have any answers. Luck should be either good or gone. He was remembering coming home once to his door ajar. He'd never forget that feeling of the world falling away from under him. That's what bad luck meant to him. What could have made him so angry that he'd wish that on someone?

Soto had turned back to Thatcher, who spoke with poison. "I can't blame you guys for instantly finding him gross. He's a slimeball."

Abby was the only one to notice that Soto's spine had stiffened at that remark.

Soto never said a word.

The younger Hispanic pressed his case: "Now, for the last time: why are you people here?"

"We ran," Meredith said simply.

Chad wiped his brow. With every word, every action, new emotions kept washing over them. They were breaking into a cold sweat trying to make sense of it all.

Abby took a chance: "We're part of a group that goes to places with...trouble."

Both Hispanics turned to regard her anew. They spoke at the same time.

Soto: "You never said..."

Thatcher: "What kind? Why?"

Chad swallowed. "There's something wrong with this town," he responded. "Getting outside is terrifying for some reason."

Thatcher frowned. "That's ridiculous."

"It's true," Soto said, turning back to the younger man. "I've been here for weeks, but couldn't get to you because I couldn't leave the house."

"But you managed to get a house," Thatcher pointed out.

"It wasn't his," Abby and Chad said together.

Meredith had her hand to her mouth. Her eyes were darting at each of them, and out the window.

"It was the one I turned to when I couldn't take it any-more. I even skidded to a stop right on the front lawn." Thatcher's eyes widened with recognition, but he didn't interrupt. "But I came here alone. So once I got inside, and found the owners were out, I had to stay." Soto clenched a fist. A bead of cold sweat travelled down the side of his head. His nostrils flared.

So many questions.

Thatcher's jaw tightened. "What did you mean when you said you found me?"

"I put you in foster care, ran, and changed my name," Soto explained.

"Guys," Meredith started.

"Why would I believe you?" Thatcher said. "My par-ents are dead."

Soto's voice was hoarse. "Your mother was missing. Reported dead. That's not the same. I don't know if she is or not, but I've been trying to find out."

"I was in the system for a decade before you showed up," Thatcher spat. "Why then? Why are you back? Did you follow me, you creep?"

"We have a prob—" Meredith tried again.

"I was involved in…" Soto sighed, gestured inartic-ulately, and tugged at one ear. "…look, I came back for you. But I had to protect you."

"You can't protect me if you're not around. Even if you are my dad — which you're not."

Uncertainty was an acid inside of everyone in the room.

"I had to be far from you to keep you safe. Look, there's a lot—"

"GUYS!" Meredith finally shouted.

Everyone turned to her.

"Don't you hear what's happening?" and she stood tall now, every bit the proud corporate professional. "Don't you smell it?"

There was a pause. Thatcher sniffed. "...smoke?"

The group looked at each other and ran upstairs. The haze as they hit the top step was a stark contrast to the sheltered basement. They went into the living room. Chad and Abby each took a curtain and pulled them wide, revealing the street to the whole of the window. Ashes were in the air. People were weeping, shouting, screaming. But there were only a few people outside.

And they were surrounded by drones.

There must have been several dozen, flitting about in a frenzied cloud.

There was a loud but dull, cracking crash.

"I've heard that sound before," Soto said. Thatcher looked at him and everyone surged with mistrust. Soto put a hand to his heart and his eyes widened even as his lips thinned to a line. His gaze fell on his son. "I knew you were gifted. This explains a lot."

Thatcher's expression was hard to read. Everyone felt tugs of confusion and curiosity.

"I've heard that sound too," Abby spoke, more against the unknown than for anyone's benefit.

Chad was getting overwhelmed, but decided to move things along: "What was it?"

"A falling beam," Soto answered quietly.

"The whole line of houses must be going up," Thatcher

mumbled as he wrestled with Soto's words. He watched as several drones disappeared to the left of his window, towards the neighbour's front door. He cursed in Spanish. "They're pulling the people out!"

Hope. Shock. Pride. A thin fear, like metal wire laced under the surface of the skin. Several of them started coughing.

"We need to get out," Meredith declared. The group moved toward the hallway and found themselves facing the front door.

Drones were flitting about outside, and several of them blared from speakers. "Can anyone make sense of that?" Chad asked.

"I'm hearing some Spanish," Thatcher said, "but there's too much noise."

A drone hovered into view through the broken door. Meredith had a thrill of recognition. "That one's from the hotel!"

Its mechanical wrist twirled and one of its fingers completed a beckoning motion. The group looked amongst each other. "Ladies first," Chad said with a grin in his mouth, not his eyes.

Meredith and Abby both stepped forward. They placed one hand in the other's and the free hand on the front door frame. Soto and Thatcher each looked upon this scene in bewilderment. Chad looked between the pairs and said to the Hispanics, "I don't get it either. But Abby has a way of coming through."

Neither man replied. Thatcher had his eyes glued on the open door, and he was sweating profusely. Everyone started to periodically cough. Soto had a flat expression and folded arms. His eyes went from Thatcher to Chad to Thatcher to the ladies and back to Thatcher, over and over.

From the drone came a female voice none of the men recognized. "All right, I'm gonna grab you now. I'm not here to hurt you, but you have to get out."

The women nodded. Gradually, they took their hands off the door frame and held them out. The drone grabbed them by the wrist. Chad could see that their held hands were becoming white at the edges.

Slowly, the drone began backing up. At first, its progress halted. The women resisted. Then it became an odd sort of wrestling match, as each woman tried to push the other forward. They never said a word, and the drone struggled not to go too much one way or the other — all while continuing to pull them out. Inch by unwilling inch, they made their way beyond the threshold.

Soto looked into the living room, since he was the only one now standing at the edge of the wall of the hallway. Edges and circles were blackening their way into the wall, and smoke was thickening with every passing second. Not far past the front step, the women disappeared into a choking fog.

Chad met Soto's eyes, and they both looked at Thatcher. He was still watching the door.

Another drone appeared in the doorway. "Hey, guys!" came an oddly cheerful male voice. "I've got some friends here. You might hear some windows breaking. Nothing personal, but we need to get you out."

"This is my house!" Thatcher declared with outrage.

Windows broke. There was a burst from the living room. Soto didn't bother to look and stopped Thatcher with a hand on his shoulder when the younger man tried to turn. Both Chad and Thatcher looked at him with venom in their eyes.

Chad shook his head and rubbed his face with one hand. Drones flew in from the back door and upstairs. Thatcher was shouting between coughs, and vainly throwing his untrained girth against Soto's honed muscles. Chad was weeping silently, and not just from the smoke. He put his back to the wall and his head in his hands.

Two drones emerged from the basement, and a female voice remarked, "That's one hell of a computer setup!"

Thatcher shook his fist at that drone, but could only cough incoherently. The hallway was filling with merciless grey. No less than three drones appeared as if coalescing out of the smoke that was the living room. They could hear the raggedness of fire. The drone in the front door was shouting. Chad dimly registered that it had been talking for a while.

The drones could no longer afford to be gentle. In a cloud, they started bullying all three men. Chad gave Soto a glance and they both nodded in agreement. Thatcher was pushing for the stairs back to the basement. They couldn't make out much of what he was saying, other than snatches like "gotta," "rig," and what might have been "life."

Soto and Chad rushed him.

Chad wasn't strong enough to force against Thatcher's sheer weight, but he was making it much more difficult for the other man to get back to the stairs. Soto was suddenly a colossus.

Icy fear gushed beneath the skin and pushed them to blindly fight for their last coherent thought. Thatcher was swarmed by two men and a group of roaring machines. The broken front door banged again and again as the cluster of humanity, both flesh and machine, fought to simply step outside.

Every second of delay was punishing their lungs. Snatches of daylight were peeking through the now billowing smoke. As heat sank into their skin, it sickened them in a claustrophobic way. It was dry but somehow sticky, as though they were drowning in the home — not the house — that melted around them.

Chad could barely register anything anymore as pure panic became his personality. From here on, it was snatches. The smoke changed, thinner but more...everywhere. How had he gotten separated? His eyes stung along with his lungs, and he had the surreal feeling that he was breathing through his blind gaze. In and out, details swirled.

Screaming, weeping, shouting, cursing, crowding. He looked up in time to see a fire truck narrowly miss a cluster of people nearby. It had at least half a dozen drones flying around it, including some of those maintenance ones that had been handling garbage. And was that a mechanical arm at the steering wheel?

More than one drone lay broken in the street. As he continued to run and stumble, he heard them. The smoke was getting a little thinner. He was beginning to see more.

A house.

He ran for it with wild abandon.

A drone crashed nearby. It had simply rained down, as if the battery had died in the air. He slammed into someone else who was running. A lanky man who stumbled heavily after the impact but, unlike Chad, kept his feet. Chad stared at the dead drone next to him, shock warring with everything else. It took him a moment to realize it wasn't the drone he mistrusted.

What did trust have to do with this?

Voices everywhere.

He'd never wanted a basement so much in his life. Anger flared from nowhere.

Chad picked himself up. He stared in wonder for a moment as he looked back the way he'd come. The entire row of houses was a centipede of orange and red hunger, wearing black smoke like a profusion of hair. The fire was ravaging two other blocks at least, from what he could see. As he made a 270 degree turn, five more drones at random intervals simply dropped.

"It's not their batteries…" he couldn't help muttering.

In the distance, past the crowd, he could see Thatcher and Soto fighting at Soto's car. Fear, rage, and something unexpected struck Chad in the spine so hard that he threw up. Even as he heaved, Thatcher was inside the car. Then Chad registered what that unexpected thing had been:

Relief.

It was short-lived: some of the people in the crowd were separating, either from drones or others in the crowd, and running back to the buildings. They were running back inside. Even as the fire spread.

The crowd's eyes were savage. They gleamed with all the wrong kinds of light. The shock of this as he got up from vomiting called him back to the urgency of escape. Dimly, he was aware of Soto's car tearing over lawns and screeching down the other street. The crowd was not people, but oozing humanity, and Chad fled in terror. He was not the only one.

An explosion in the distance didn't much register, but shortly afterward some clattering made him look up as he ran. It was the drone that had helped Thatcher out of the front door, and it had hit the ground at an angle.

Chad stopped for a coughing fit. But the crash of the drone had gotten through his panic enough to make him look around. Not ten feet away, there she was.

"Abby!" he rasped out a shout.

She was on her motorbike, in her bike gear, and looking around. She flipped up her visor when she caught sight of him. Her eyes were wide and a little too still. Chad was running, stumbling, heaving, arms flailing in his desperation. He didn't quite reach her before she turned around and gunned her engine.

She was out of the diner's lot by the time he scrambled into the car. His door was still swinging, the alarm demanding a seatbelt, when he hit the gas. They were out of town, Abby well ahead of him, when he remembered his phone. He tore it out as he drove, swerving a little past the centre line while he checked it.

Seven missed messages, all but one from Tasha.

One missed call from Victor.

"F-," he started, and lost the rest of the word to a coughing fit. Looking up through cough-teared eyes, he could see Abby's shoulders rack and heave. Her hand went up to wipe at her visor.

They both pulled over. Chad opened his door, sitting sideways with his feet on the ground. He wept openly, holding his phone out for Abby. She swung off her bike, lifting her visor up. She'd sprayed it with spit from coughing while she was rushing to get it on. As she absently relieved Chad of his phone, her eyes were on the town.

Smoke clouds outgrew and outnumbered the clouds of drones, which were in a flurry. There were little pops and bursts as buildings collapsed on themselves and various things — like BBQ propane tanks in back yards — were exposed to the unchecked fire.

Meredith was dead centre in the crowd. She watched a drone get caught by three members of the mob, who tilted it downward and proceeded to slam it, camera first, into the street. Only a few minutes after the car containing the two Hispanics had roared away, everything had shifted. That nameless urgency had vanished. Everyone else, though, was filling a vacuum. She could see it: they'd lived with whatever had been here, and now that it was gone, the hole needed filling.

She watched the windows of a house let out a scintillating scream, but couldn't tell what made them explode.

Soto's wild driving began to ease once they got out of town. They were on the highway by the time Chad and Abby left the diner's lot. "In through your nose," he said, "and out through your mouth."

Thatcher was huddled into himself, coughing and wiping at tears and mucus. "What?"

"Focus on your breathing," Soto said through a half-suppressed cough. His fitness meant that he didn't struggle as much with the smoke damage.

"F-," Thatcher started, and coughed again. *My rig. My life. All of it. All I have are my clothes!*

"Breathe in. Count for six seconds. In. Breathe in. There you go," Soto continued to coach as he drove. It was keeping his hands steady on the steering wheel. "In for six. Hold two. Out for four. Mouth. Out of your mouth. Start again. In six. Use your nose. I know it's hard right now, but just focus on this. There's nothing else. Nose six. Hold two. Mouth four." He continued this litany for almost forty-five minutes, interrupting whenever Thatcher tried to speak or do anything else.

The routine was hindered by their coughing. They'd need attention. Soto noticed in the rear-view mirror that emergency vehicles from a nearby town were heading out. They must have caught word of the disaster. "You've kidnapped me," Thatcher said, but he found he just couldn't muster the rage he wanted. He stared at the man he'd known as Geronimo, unblinking and resentful, and wanted very much not to have to keep following this breathing routine.

"I've saved your life," Soto corrected. He was exhaustion in human form. "Agoraphobia is a slow poison."

Thatcher was watching the windshield, no longer paying attention to the road. On the windshield was a scratch, most likely from something they'd plowed through in their panicked escape. He stared at it. "I don't have any phobias," he bit out.

"The whole town had it. I had it when I came, that's why I couldn't get to you sooner."

They argued about what happened for hours, and argued more when Soto refused to go to a hospital or a hotel, but insisted they'd need medical attention. Food. Rest.

"What's your plan, then?" Thatcher demanded.

Author's Note: *This story introduces my character Thatcher, from the* Knives of Engen *series. It was written before* Diary of Knives *and released in the* Undead/ Rebirth *collection. I've included it here for anyone who missed the collection or would like to know about the Towerton incident referenced in* Diary of Knives. *Naturally, it is also a good fit for the themes and motifs around which I've structured this anthology.*

COLD COMFORTS

"It worked!" she said, and her joy was mingled with sadness.

"Then come through!" he insisted, frustrated and afraid. "The Republic is safe, and even Nana is comfortable. The light is so warm! Come through!"

All he could see was blackness on the surface of the ice.

She stood in a dimly lit bed chamber. Her chamber. The mirror was set into an alcove, in vogue when the family mansion was built. The design was now outdated, but he knew the room. Black walls, fashioned from obsidian, were a solid shadow to him and a shimmering bedroom of igneous glass to her.

Again she stood before the ornate pearl-backed mirror and looked upon her brother in a world of vibrant colour with a star so alive it must have had a pulse. Their world, consumed by the Ice, lay in wait on the other side of her bedroom door. She placed her hand on the mirror. "Was this surface here when you stepped through?"

"What?" he asked, fighting back a mounting panic.

"We stepped through. Of course it wasn't there."

Absently, she nodded. "Then it's true…"

"Come through!"

"Brother…" and she fought with all her dying world to appear to him as a soul that had peace, control, and belonging "…the Ice has frozen the space between time."

His skin was like an ocean without currents, and his blood became stone. "Sister…!"

But even voice froze.

At least she couldn't be as awake as she looked.

WINTER TRIANGLE

"They used to have sages for these places," Sovan grouched as quietly as he could. He was climbing a set of laroc shelving, scouring the books. Laroc was a kind of artificial coral, grown indoors to form basic structures like pillars or — in this case — bookshelves. Under misleading light, Sovan was fairly certain these were beige, though they had striations like veins of ore that had signature colours. This laroc bookshelf was one of many, though few remained as anything more than rubble or tipped half-walls. Surfaces were worn smooth, and the curvaceous edges had a stone-like coarseness in their texture.

Spanning disjointed sheaves, the lighting here was uneven and came from holes or cracks in what was once a vaulting ceiling. Well, most of one; its dome-like architecture abruptly became a solid and rigid line of stone. At least, that's what Sovan could make of it in the dimness. Most of the place was a wreck, with scattered surviving books little more than pageless rot. Puddles of moss, fungus, water, and something else dotted the floors. That something else, Sovan guessed, was produced by a thing that was lurking in the area. His voice hadn't echoed.

::You know I can hear your thoughts, right?:: asked a voice in his head. It came from a spider nestled on the span of muscle between his shoulder and neck. His name was Glimpse, and he was spectral. Translucent white-blue, producing no light of his own, he was easy to overlook; he was noticed like a web in the half-light out of the corner of the eye. He tapped an incorporeal leg, about the length of a pen, on Sovan's neck. ::We haven't seen what's in here yet!::

::I'm allowed to mutter to myself,:: Sovan thought back at Glimpse as he shuffled and sidled. He moved along the bookshelves with a spider's intuition, and even enjoyed some enhancement of his grip and control over friction with surfaces as he climbed. He checked the spines of most books. Some he had to pull out because the spine was worn or, for some reason, unlabelled.

His efforts were efficient and swift, but also tense. There were sounds, mostly spongy clatters, coming from somewhere in this large room. He imagined sandstone boots making such a sound. Spine, spine, cover, spine, cover. Glimpse leapt off of him and hopped over to the bookshelf on the other side of the aisle whenever they reached a place where the shelves were intact on both sides.

There were other shuffles in the distance. It might have been the sounds of workers moving freight if it weren't for the complete lack of speech. Most of the smells were plants, moulds, and a scent like calcium that came from the laroc. Glimpse landed on his back, and that was enough contact — even through clothes — to think at his companion. ::We should at least have looked for some kind of map or signage for how the library's organized.:: Glimpse didn't need a physical form in order to convey his frisson of disquiet.

Sovan sighed. ::We've been over this. They used different systems in each—:: His full attention was on the book he'd just pulled out. *The Principle Edges and Their Sub-types: An Introduction*. This was it! He climbed — proud of his silence — to the top of the bookshelf. He'd chosen a particularly opaque stretch of shadow and visually swept the room as he mentally discussed with Glimpse.

::You really can't just give it to her, you know,:: the spider thought while Sovan packed the book into a thin backpack strapped tightly to his torso.

::Why not?:: Sovan was appreciating the sheer scale of the library he'd found. It was easy to miss. When the three floating continents had crashed, this was one of many buildings to slide into newly created ravines, valleys, drained lakes, and other such catastrophes. A colossal promontory, slivered from the edge of the (in this case) rock-hewn valley, had slid over the top of the broken domed roof of the library. That was their guess, at any rate, based on what they'd found of the building on the outside. Between this and how the building wedged into the wall, the central room appeared far taller than would really make much sense.

Glimpse, less impressed, continued with the conversation. ::You've sold to her before. It's hard enough to make ends meet without word getting out that we don't have to charge a premium for a rescued book.::

::Don't you think it's weird…:: Sovan mused, untroubled by his companion's argument, ::...this building is a bit tucked away, but you'd think there'd be people.::

::Don't dodge the question.:: Glimpse would have wagged a finger if he had one.

::I'm not. We have some coin. Besides, I want to see where she goes with those Edges of hers.::

::I think you want to be a part of her comings and goings. And there are people. You can hear them. Look at the way the holes in the ceiling have been worked. They're all angled, so the weather that does get this far gets pushed into walls or corners. Those sculpted curves in the rock face and old walls are like gutters. Daylight gets through, but some of the holes are covered up and there are skeletons on the floor below them! It's like the place is coordinated, designed after the cataclysm. In fact...::

Hairs raised on the back of Sovan's neck as he registered all this purposeful work. Yes, there were patches of green or brownish growths of mosses, grasses, ferns, and fungi. Yes, there were water puddles. But even the collapsed shelving was suspiciously either too clear or far more blocked-up than—

A fleshy psithurism was all the warning he needed. Sovan didn't bother looking, but crouched in a flash and launched his body away. He cast a glance over his shoulder as he jumped from his landing spot on the railing of broken stairs near the full-storey-high bookshelf he'd been on a moment before. ::Not here!:: Glimpse thought. And he was right; Sovan was sliding and scrabbling down the wall because it was slimy in the half-dark. The surprise had stopped him from picking out proper purchase.

Standing where he'd been a moment before was a bizarre, six-legged monstrosity. At the ends of its armoured legs were wriggling...somethings. Only a part of the creature was visible, since Sovan had specifically chosen that spot for how dark it was. The creature was able to span the distance between shelves with ease, and they'd never have supported its gargantuan weight if they weren't made from such robust material. The legs and (torso? thorax?) were coated in a mottled spongiform carapace. It might have been a living industrial platform, were it not for the obviously predatory behaviour.

Most disturbing of all were three engorged distensions, something like a blend of ganglia and antennae. Arms made out of brain. The abomination seemed large enough to eat an entire caravan. Maybe Sovan had miscounted the legs? Darkness and his full-bore sprinting could add to numbers and spans.

::We need Skelter,:: Sovan thought at Glimpse.

::Let's get somewhere safe before letting our minds wander, champ,:: the spectral spider replied.

::Champ?:: Sovan allowed himself some amusement as he hopped over large boulders of laroc blocking an aisle of shelves. Like broken seashells, they were shockingly sharp on their broken edges.

Both of them were shocked that the ponderous creature made such good time spanning the flat stretch of floor between the broken staircase and the set of damaged bookshelves Sovan was now climbing. Though its central mass was a bulbous, armoured sack as large as a merchant's wagon, its legs could propel it with thunderous force once it had solid ground to accommodate its frame.

::Did you notice the clouds it's making?:: Glimpse

asked.

Sovan hadn't. As soon as he'd run enough of the length of the bookshelf to cut off a direct line of sight to the abomination, he gracefully slipped over the edge and climbed on all fours along the shelving. ::What am I missing?:: Sovan asked.

::It's been firing off some kind of spore-sack-things from its feet. They all land at what I think are exits, holes, or alcoves. Then they burst into thick green dust.::

Sovan reached the end of the aisle and climbed over the rubble that formed an endcap. His grip was impressive and the climbing knowledge he gained from his connection to Glimpse did a lot for him, but he couldn't just stick to a flat surface. He needed *some* foothold. ::Should w—:: he began.

Many things happened at once: the shelves shook with oddly timed and gargantuan footfalls; people spilled into the library from the rough directions of those entrances Glimpse had mentioned; Sovan slipped around the other side of the bookshelf he was leaning against; and a ganglion loomed down to him from the top. Its timing and direction were perfect; somehow, it knew exactly where he was. He saw no eyes. He'd been careful about the noise of his movement or breathing, even at a short run.

::Kill it, then I'll get us up the wall,:: Glimpse thought.

The thing seemed to be handing Sovan the target of a brain-like appendage. All too easy. He braced himself for how the soft flesh would feel around his hand. He never wore gloves because they'd interfere with the climbing enhancements he gained from Glimpse. He transferred one of his knives from its sheath on his right hip into the semi-fungal brain bulge.

White.

White.

White.

A humming kind of pain smeared his consciousness back into the present. It was a mental pain, as though all his thoughts and memories were a body that had smashed into the surface of water after hundreds of feet of falling. He was alone, staring at the broken and jarringly blended wall and rock plate above. It was impossibly far away, and the bookshelf stood ahead of him. It was monolithic now; any one of the books was easily four times his height.

Noise came to him as though his skull were full of marshmallows. A mob? But they weren't calling out. Just the sounds of running, falling, grappling, collisions, and crowded chase. Dull, hulking splats indicated the gait of the creature in the distance. Sovan realized that Glimpse was gone. He looked at his raised hands. Pale blue-white, the edges of his body seemingly stitched into the reality around him rather than having a boundary of their own.

Sovan hastened to his feet, got to the edge of the book-shelf, and jumped straight up. Being in spectral form, he didn't so much have gravity as attachment to surfaces. So he continued up. Speed was greater in this form because there was no air resistance or weight, but it was a different kind of velocity. He was less an arrow than a jet of smoke. Once he reached the top of the bookshelf, he grabbed the edge before he could float off toward the ceiling. He stopped instantly; there was no inertia.

The creature was on the opposite end of the massive room, though he couldn't see it directly. It seemed to be caught up in the crowd of...people? It was hard to tell from here; he only had sound to go by, as the bookshelves extended before him with chasms between them.

Glimpse's body, now a blend of blacks and browns, was covered in a red muck. He was making good time across the gaps. Of the armed spider variety, Glimpse had legs that were all the same length and spaced out the same way. They typically kept a heightened bend, so that it looked like his cephalothorax was low and surrounded by skittering arches. He was monumentally large; to become corporeal, the spider had had to take on the same amount of mass Sovan's body had possessed.

Glimpse turned on his arrival to offer a rear leg. It didn't have any of the red muck. Sovan grabbed it, wondering why that muck clearly mattered, and found himself in his original form.

::RUN!:: the spider yelled in his mind.

He ran.

The creature was atop the bookshelves again. The mob, Sovan saw between broken gaps in the shelving, was clambering and scrambling in a seething mass. There was still a red smear ahead of them, fallen from Glimpse when he'd gone spectral again. But it was the mob that shocked him more; they were humans, rightly enough. They looked at once incredibly strong and horribly sick, emaciated and gaunt. Vicious and animalistic.

::What's going on?:: Sovan demanded as he climbed, jumped, ran, swapped forms and back again, and grabbed a book at random.

::Later,:: Glimpse replied. ::For now, watch out for the red goop that thing...shoots? Spits? The mob didn't start doing much until that red muck hit me, then they went for me with hate.::

Sovan cast back glances whenever he got a chance. One of the creature's legs was...out of tune? Lazy? Off in some way. The abomination covered the red muck in some of the sticky goo he'd noticed in puddles when he first got here. One of the ganglia was flimsy, awkward, and oozing fluids. Sovan produced web from his hand, on the book, and threw it. The book carried the webbing, which he strove to produce quickly so it wouldn't slow the book too much, and it flew over the railing of a balcony on what would have been a second floor. It wedged between the handle and spokes of the railing, and Sovan leapt from the bookshelf. He began climbing the web like a rope.

::Have I ever told you that you're a madman?:: Glimpse asked.

::I talk to a spider every day,:: Sovan answered with a grin.

Climbing the rope, he was an obvious target. Still, it hurt more than he'd expected as the red muck slammed his back like a bully driving down on a smaller child. It was imposing pressure that left him breathless, and it ground him into the wall in front of him. He compelled himself upward, past the stars in his eyes and the full-body echo of crushing force. Another burst, this one white, splattered beside him. He didn't know what it did until one of his feet slid on that part of the wall as he rushed himself up.

His foot shot down; it was like he'd tried to run on ice.

::That's how it got me with the muck the first time,::

Glimpse remarked.

Most of the mental math for what had happened after his white-out was coming together, but now wasn't the time for his remaining questions. ::Now!:: Sovan thought.

They swapped.

Now corporeal, Glimpse finished the climb with ease and grabbed the wedged book, crouching at the base of the railing. He then spooled up the web, now covered in most of the free-falling muck, and attached it to one side of the book. On the other, he wove fresh web. Spurts of muck landed here and there. At such a distance, height, and angle, however, the creature was having trouble aiming.

Sovan, meanwhile, climbed the wall in his shrunken spectral form until he crested the top and clambered onto the spider's back. A quick glance revealed that this balcony was isolated by rubble, broken wall, and collapsed floor.

Glimpse could climb them out.

::That thing and its...uh, mob, will chase us,:: Sovan thought, and outlined his plan.

Glimpse was careful not to let the muck touch his body, so one of his legs was held away from him and kept the webbed book aloft. He scurried up the wall and did what Sovan, even with borrowed abilities, could not: he walked on the ceiling as easily as though it were a floor or wall.

They were so high at this point that the mob had begun to disperse. Some of them, attracted by a bluish fluid the thing managed to get on itself, were trying to help it with the damaged ganglion. Sovan realized he was still missing his knife. Were they trying to extract it?

Glimpse got directly above and dropped the webbed book, fresh web down. Stuck shut, the bundle was heavy enough not to sway in the air; it landed directly on the back of the creature and stuck there.

With the red muck exposed to the air, the creatures trying to help it started tearing into the wounded append-age. The thing made quivering, squelching bleats of dis-tress. Slowly, its captured people began turning on it until the mob became a tide. Except for the ones tearing at its ganglion, they were largely harmless and trampled.

They were also occupied.

The pair didn't wait to watch how the whole situation played out; Glimpse scampered for the hole in the ceiling through which they'd entered. Soon Sovan was traipsing over rubble-strewn grass glimmering with the early red-gold of sunset.

::Charge extra,:: Glimpse thought.

::I've never known you to grumble,:: Sovan said. He chuckled out loud, then looked around. No sign of any-one. Yet he crept as often as not. The dark of night had be-come its own kind of web when the Winter Triangle — the floating continents of the High Magic — had fallen. Trees, rocks, turned-over wagons, abandoned shelters ranging from tents to stone wayhouses, and any other shelter they could manage provided cover until they could get to their camp with Skelter. Sometimes Glimpse would take over.

::Are you really that much stealthier than I am, or do you just like the fresh air and the evening sun?:: Sovan objected.

::What's this? Grumbling?:: The spider didn't have the

equipment for a smirk, but the impression of his thoughts felt like one.

They arrived at the "cave" he and Skelter had chosen for the night. In truth, it was the hollowed-out husk of some creature Sovan had never seen before. There was too much bone for it to have been a turtle, and too much opalescence to be mere bone. Sovan rounded one of the large, empty cocoons that partially concealed its entrance and there she was. Skelter stood with her arms folded over a padded doublet with some sections of hardened leather and a few well-placed studs over vital areas, as well as the shoulders and elbows. Except for some chain, the rest of her outfit was similar. It was mostly grey and brown, and she wore gloves with studs on the knuckles. A double-ended mace was strapped to her back.

Her hair was river-clean and kept short, but completely unstyled. Sovan had that thinking in common with her; they couldn't be worried about salon quality on the road, and long hair made no sense for freelancers or mercenaries. Her eyes were viridian, an unusually dark shade of green. "I told you to wait here for me."

"Yeah, well, you're not the only one who's been looking around," Sovan replied. Too gruff? She respected strength, though.

Glimpse had leapt from Sovan's shoulder to one of the cocoons and was now climbing it. Sovan was grateful for the discretion. Skelter rolled her eyes at Sovan. Drat. "I don't want to waste rations if we don't have to. Are you up to some hunting and gathering?" She looked him up and down. Her expression was...complicated. Was that a good thing?

"I just need a short rest. My clothes took more punishment than I did," Sovan said as the pair of them sat at the entrance to the cave. They needed to be on the same wall to gain the full benefit of the shelter of the cocoons; the pair would see before being seen if someone showed up. Skelter's crossbow was loaded, with her bolt quiver nearby, and set on a rock that would take advantage of this arrangement.

As she sat, one inch too many for easy contact, she regarded him with a critical eye. "Lots of bumps, scrapes, and bruises, for all that." Her words were a rebuke, but not hostile. She rubbed her head a few times.

"I'll tell you what I was doing if you tell me what you were doing," he said with his best grin as he took off his pack and began getting himself sorted. He arranged his clothes, checked his wounds, and drained the last of his water skin.

"I told you," Skelter replied, "getting us a job for the road. We're near enough to where Chantice crashed, but we'll need to be prepared."

"Don't we have everything we need? We're not expecting any more towns, at least not with living people. I wish we had more on the Phantom Host, though."

Skelter lifted her brows. "That's fortunate."

Sovan watched her face. Then he blinked. "You didn't."

"They're actually pretty good negotiators. We'll be getting silver pieces and diamond dust, much easier to trade with in the nearest communities. Plus some knowledge about them." Skelter's shoulders were a little lower than usual, and she sometimes pressed her thumbs against both sides of the top of her nose. Her tone was satisfied, and her head was high.

"You took a job from the army of the dead!?" Sovan's gaze shot around the cave and the entrance as though he thought they might be summoned by the conversation.

"Don't worry, I didn't consent." She meant joining the Phantom Host; they could not add an unwilling deceased person to their ranks.

"Why are they hiring?" Sovan was suspicious. He adjusted his clothing, made up of reinforced cloth with some leather arm and leg bracing. His shoes were particularly important, and he made sure they didn't show too much wear as he tightened some of the laces. All of his equipment was designed for silence, range of motion, and lightweight travel. He glanced around for Glimpse, but the spectral spider was probably keeping watch until called.

"Did you know they came from the ocean?" Skelter asked.

Sovan frowned. "From the depths? Or across the sea?"

Skelter shrugged. "Both? Not sure. But Seerie fell while it was over the ocean." The Winter Triangle were three floating continents that had crashed a few years ago: Chantice, Seerie, and Beetlejewel. "Every network I've tapped has traced the Phantom Host to the coastlines. Two of the southern capitals have already sworn their kingdoms to the Host. They're moving like an empire. They're colonizing."

"So you took an imperial job?"

"Pretty much." She'd never been as troubled about the undead as most other people. They needed consent to increase their army, and more people joined them than some expected, but they couldn't just take all the lands of the living by force. Skelter was simply being practical.

"Can we expect them at Chantice?"

"You know they can't enter any part of the Triangle."

"Do I?" Sovan pressed. "That's what people say, sure, but everything changed when the Winter Triangle crashed. What do we really know?"

Skelter stood. "We'll want to get food before it gets too dark. I'll lay out the job in the morning. What were you doing?"

Sovan collected himself, withdrew the book as he stood, and shouldered his pack. "This should help with your headaches." He began walking and whistled so that Glimpse would join him.

::Smooth,:: the spider said as soon as it landed on his shoulder.

::Hey, she's one of a kind. I can't just show up with flowers and invite her to the festival of—::

"I can't take this!"

Sovan stopped at the sound of Skelter's voice and turned to find that she hadn't moved. There were now twelve feet between them. He was nearing the crossbow, as they liked to take thresholds carefully. He didn't know what to say.

"The right buyer would pay our retirement for this. I can't afford it," Skelter went on.

"You can't afford to keep all that energy in your head, either," Sovan said. "If you don't learn to use your Edge, it'll kill you."

She'd begun flipping pages and consulting indices and

glossaries even as she wandered in the direction of the crossbow. "I could study what I need, then fence it..."

"Pretty sure you're gonna want to keep that, at least until you've mastered it. What did you do with the Edge-work Energy Primer?" Sovan watched her with consternation. He'd hoped for some small measure of contact. Maybe not a hug (not her way), but a nudge. A hand on the shoulder. Sitting a little closer.

She snapped the book closed and held it up with one hand, staring at her crossbow and thinking. Sliding *The Principle Edges* into her own pack, she turned to regard Sovan. They were only two feet apart now. "I sold it and gave the money to my family before I left. For now, it's enough to keep them holed up. They've started making plans, but their fleet, wagons, stalls, and stores were all destroyed or confiscated when the Phantom Host came flooding in."

Sovan was drained from his efforts and would have been just as happy collapsing into sleep without a meal. He'd sooner go back to that creature than admit this to Skelter, so he nodded acknowledgement of her words and started out of the cave. "Fair enough. Let's move out, maybe set up camp on the way to the job."

That snapped Skelter out of her amazement. "Wait, why would we do that?" She caught him up without difficulty.

::You should let me take over,:: Glimpse thought. ::I'm not exhausted, and I'll be able to hunt easier.::

"Oh, I had some stumbling blocks while in this buried library a few hours' march that way." He pointed for Skelter and thought at Glimpse, ::I wouldn't be able to talk, and I don't gain rest while spectral.::

Skelter narrowed her eyes. She gripped the strap of her pack protectively, as if she thought she might have to give it up. "What happened?"

Glimpse replied to Sovan's thoughts. ::I'm worried — when you stabbed that thing, you started looking like its drones. You got all stretched, discoloured, and weird in the face.::

Sovan wanted to play it cool and not have anyone worry, but he was tired and she wouldn't be put off easily. Nor was she slow of wit. So he sighed, conveyed Glimpse's commentary where his memory got fuzzy, and explained what had happened.

Skelter paled, looked every which way, and took him across the road they'd just reached. She plunged them into the brush, perpendicular to the road and in the opposite direction of where they'd come. The road swerved away wide on their far right, but she kept them going. Sovan was too tired to argue. "That was a knowpox!" she declared in a harsh whisper. They'd been going long enough that he was starting to think she wouldn't explain herself.

::I've heard of those in stores or alleys while you were occupied with your book selling,:: Glimpse commented. Sovan narrowed his eyes but couldn't recall the word.

Skelter elaborated: "They feed off your knowledge and memory, and nest close to big roads. Anywhere that gets a lot of traffic but few people stopping for long. That way, no one comes looking when one or two people go missing. My parents made me do lots of lessons for their merchant stuff, but I was more about boats and the sea. I learned, though. You have no idea how lucky you are to have Glimpse."

::Sounds about right.::

::Quiet, you.::

::Is that any way to thank your spider and saviour? Lord and spider? Wait, wait, I can make this work.::

Ignoring some of his spectral companion's banter, Sovan tried to focus his thoughts on the matter at hand. It was like being mentally cross-eyed. "Is that why we're so far in the wrong way?::

"Obviously," she said. "...and you're gonna need lots of rest. Let me guess: you're finding it hard to keep it together? Everything seems slimy and slow? You have a craving for mushrooms, and you're thinking that that creature really wasn't so bad as all that?"

Sovan stared with open astonishment.

"It'll wear off. There's been time to study what they do to you because some of the nests have been dug out and... purged. I'm in charge of hunting for tonight. And swap to Glimpse until it's time to sleep."

::Heh heh, told you.:: Glimpse's mind radiated triumph.

::You're just trying to stir me up because you're jealous she's proud of me.::

Glimpse stayed quiet on that one. The feelings Sovan sensed from him were mixed. Curious.

Skelter took the lead for the remainder of the night. She made and coated them in something that was good for throwing off their trail from knowpox. The humans ate fresh venison and Sovan stayed near the fire Skelter had set up while Glimpse saw to his own needs. Sovan and Glimpse treated each other's diets and needs the way

Sovan and Skelter handled going to the washroom. Privacy, no judgment, and stay nearby in case of trouble were the basic rules.

As soon as Sovan's consciousness came back from the unfeeling darkness of sleep, he knew he'd slept in. He hopped up in alarm. Skelter didn't seem to notice. She was so deep into her book she might have been reading it with her spinal cord. He supposed that made sense; her mental energy had been building past a healthy threshold without a way to release it for weeks. Then, in the span of a breath, she and the forest around them rapidly grew to gigantic proportions.

Glimpse had taken the opportunity to get himself a body and rest in it the moment Sovan had gotten in his R&R. Skelter didn't leave used mess kits or uneaten food lying around. That was an obvious way to draw the attention of things with teeth and other, less savoury parts. Sovan wouldn't need breakfast while he was spectral, so he took watch. That was the system they'd worked out.

No sign of any knowpox. Sovan still couldn't believe all that Skelter had told him. What else did she know about? What else had she seen or overcome? Once he'd planned out his perimeter, he circled it inward, looking for signs of activity. He hid in a bush on a narrow road. It was an offshoot, like a tributary, and not frequented nearly enough to be of interest to knowpox or their bandit-like drones. Sovan watched a group of skeletal Phantom Host pulling a wagon.

Was it enough to be hidden from vision? He was spectral at the moment. The Phantom Host weren't new, exactly; they'd been colonizing the continent for a few months. Nevertheless, they didn't put up posters of their weaknesses. This particular setup was a common sight for the Host's operations. They seemed to have some unusual creations that might have been magical or some kind of technological, but nothing like the animal magics of Chantice or the armories of Beetlejewel. So when something needed moving, they had two basic options: pulleys and such, or tireless members of the Host.

The wagon they pulled was full of lumber and a few strapped-in boxes. There were six skeletons wearing hardened leather suits. Metal was too precious and rare to be used as armour, and it didn't benefit the Host all that much anyway. These suits mostly prevented the skeletons from getting ropes, handles, crossbars, sticks, and the like stuck between their bones. They ran, in two lines of three, pushing wooden handles that connected to a central hitching bar. No muscles meant no fatigue, and their motions were unnervingly mechanical.

They didn't seem to care much about their surroundings.

If Sovan were corporeal, he'd have worked out how to attack or sabotage the group. Life was important to him in a way that made the Phantom Host a horror to him. He didn't think it was a coincidence that the Host showed up out of the ocean. Some time after the floating continents had fallen, one of them lost to the ocean.

Sovan went back to camp. It was probably for the best; even if he had attacked, it would have been noticed sooner or later. Unwanted attention came all too easily these days.

He made his way back uneventfully. While there were

no signs of human or Host activity, they had to be mind-ful of the forest itself. Many of the magical powers, equip-ment, and creatures that had made the Winter Triangle so influential were either gone, re-purposed, or running amok.

Skelter specifically chose this site because there were vampire trees in a line blocking off much of the south and west. Once their roots were down, they looked like their surrounding species. Spruce, in this case. They were best used as shelter after a recent feeding, since it took them weeks to digest captured prey. This included the Phantom Host, which vampire trees particularly fed upon (when rooted) or attacked (when uprooted).

Sovan stopped a few feet from Skelter. Her book was lying open on a rock beside her, and she was staring at nothing. He watched her for a while, but this wasn't just a case of a wandering mind. If he stepped into her peripher-al vision, she might lose her concentration. A while longer he stood, searching for Glimpse. There was no obvious sign of the spider.

Finally, she came to herself, blinking many times as she took in her surroundings. Sovan couldn't speak in this form, and Glimpse could only communicate with the man while they were touching. So the two humans used a few simple hand gestures they'd worked out: Host nearby, no problems at camp, Glimpse is that way.

They were soon travelling again. Glimpse had be-come spectral and rode Sovan's shoulder. "I'd kill for some horses. The Host can't use them, and we don't have them!" Sovan said.

"Honestly, we're more likely to get where we're going

without beasts working for us. It would get the attention of the Host's sentries," Skelter replied distantly.

"Speaking of, where *are* we going?" Sovan spoke as jovially as he could.

"Why don't you talk about your family?" she asked, suddenly coming back to the moment.

Sovan was taken aback. ::Make something up,:: Glimpse suggested.

"I was in one of the lands that outlawed planting or keeping vampire trees," Sovan answered. "My family were part of a political resistance because they suspected that the king was enacting Host rule to keep his power while effectively surrendering to the Host. A group of both living and dead razed the hideout while I was on my way back from selling a black-market tome. They took my family right out from under me."

::That was the opposite of making something up.::

::She's too smart to believe that I'm wandering a country under siege from imperial undead because I have nothing better to do,:: Sovan quipped.

Skelter was silent for a little while. Sovan appreciated that she didn't try to offer up condolences. He couldn't have explained the gratitude, but Glimpse understood, and who else would need to know? Eventually, as though there hadn't been a lapse in conversation, she said, "The job is to take an asset out of the hands of a Host position just past that." She pointed at a rocky promontory in the distance, covered in greying grass.

It took them two and a half days of long marches to approach the landmark. During that time, the trio alternated watches, rested, and chatted. Skelter talked about her upbringing in a merchant's guild, and how she'd been considering the military as a way of getting to the sea. She'd privately entertained thoughts of piracy but hadn't told her parents that much.

During the group's various breaks, she continued with her odd staring sessions while reading, studying, or holding a meal in her lap, or just...sitting.

Glimpse and Sovan, meanwhile, joked or chatted privately and sometimes attempted to bring Skelter in on that. She couldn't hear the spider's thoughts. The duo were more or less happy looking for ways to get back at the Host and living their days. Sovan had stolen Glimpse from the remnants of Chantice and set all the creatures loose, which had seemed a jolly grand idea at the time. For reasons that were probably unrelated, Sovan was banned from the Barony of Taront.

The morning after they'd camped near a clearing facing the promontory had begun with a shock for Glimpse, who was corporeal at the time. Sovan had been watching in the opposite direction and came running after the most bizarre splashing sound he'd ever heard. They'd camped near a pond, and Sovan floated onto the scene of Glimpse running circles around Skelter while she stood...on her tiptoes?

No.

After weeks of increasing strain from the energy of her Edge, the relief was as much in her posture as her newly smoothed face. A thick puddle-bog situation spanned a broad area before her, one end of it leaking into a crater Sovan realized was a now half-filled pond.

"I did it!" Skelter declared.

Despite pressing her, however, a now-corporeal Sovan couldn't get much more out of her. They soon looked across at the promontory. It was high, broad, and oddly tilted. They were broaching the outskirts of where Beetlejewel had crashed. The far, far outskirts, of course; a flying continent makes for an impressive impact zone. Down a long dusty road to their left, four massive suits of empty armour were moving in no particular pattern with no obvious purpose. The trio hid behind an overturned construction of what looked like metal-banded laroc. It had been a magical machine once, operated by crystals that were now shattered and dim.

They hid behind it until they were sure the Havoc Suits wouldn't notice them, then they made their way slowly across the road to the promontory. It was stressful going slowly, but they didn't want to stir up dust that might be noticed after they'd passed.

::Let's come at this from another angle,:: Glimpse suggested. ::Ask her…::

"…what are we getting paid for this job?"

"The asset," she said with a gleam. "Come on!" and she began climbing the steep, grey-grassy slope.

Sovan went with it, and soon passed her. He was lighter, more fleet-footed, and more comfortable on all fours. The grass, he was disquieted to discover, was cold to the touch. Any terrain held by the Phantom Host for long enough began to show these signs. Despite her own discomfort, Skelter joined him lying on their bellies as they looked over the edge.

Sovan became aware that (a) his mouth had been agape for far too long and (b) Skelter was rummaging through her pack. Below them was a fully armed and mobilized garrison of the Phantom Host. More than that, there were buildings and walkways built of wood, stone, and even laroc. That last was somewhat cruder, as they had to lump together whatever laroc had survived the continental crash; no one knew how to make it now. Most of all of this was a carrack, a sea-faring vessel of (in this case) three masts. Its sails were spectral, and it was flying!

Sovan turned to Skelter and his words died on his lips. She'd tied a length of her rope around her waist and was bundling up the rope enough to hand it over to him. "Tie on," she said.

His mouth moved, but no sound came out.

::There are spiders that can toss their web up to fly, you know,:: Glimpse remarked in Sovan's head.

Then it all came together.

"You can't be serious," Sovan said.

She shoved him and began tying the rope for him. "Quickly!" she said. "That's not a large window of opportunity!" She'd spent her young life handling countless kinds of ships and boats in all manner of weather. Her muscles were not in the habit of negotiation.

"They have a garrison! Right there!" Sovan had rapidly switched his motions to cooperation and wasn't so much arguing as marveling. "But how will the ro—"

"Hang on!" she said as she scrunched her face.

::The way I understand it, you can't go back once you shape your mental energy for an Edge,:: Glimpse mused.

::THAT'S your take-away!? WE'RE FLYING!:: Sovan mentally burst out.

That was a generous way of putting it; both of them

had to cling to the length of rope in front of them for dear life. Skelter was artlessly yanking the other end of the rope so that it flew them up to the...sky carrack? Sovan was higher up the length and would be the first to crest whatever ledge or rail they'd reach. He dared not say anything and kept the full force of his gaze on the vessel. Don't distract her, don't distract her, don't distra—

They flew over the railing of the stern and collapsed in a heap. As they rushed to unrope themselves, Sovan said in a coarse whisper, "I'm loving the idea of taking the Host down a peg, but we're a little high up for that!"

"This is a test flight," she said back, "and we're alone on this deck. If they didn't hear us land, they won't hear us talk. They only have plans for a crew of five, including the pilot."

"How do you know that?" Sovan said, doing his best to put a bit of smooth confidence into his tone.

"The factions of the Host take their rivalry seriously. Now: you get rid of the pilot and try to take over. I'll get the others."

"What? How?"

Skelter ran the length of the deck.

::What are you waiting for?::

Scowling at the spider on his back, Sovan spanned the deck in an awkward series of lunges, jumps, dashes, and four-limbed semi-climbs. The pilot, it seemed, was having some trouble with controlling a massive sea-going vessel that was somehow in the sky.

Go figure.

Skelter had her sea legs, which seemed to work well enough for the sky, but went prone and wrapped her arms around the rails of the banister overlooking the quarter-deck. She scrunched her face. Sovan arrived beside her in time to see that there were three of the Host on board. These were distended and barbarous in appearance; some of the bulkier people, once they'd consented to join the Phantom Hose after death, were allowed to bloat in their decomposition before being...recruited. They resembled the old stories about trolls. Sort of.

Two of them were working on a ballista. Most likely for testing purposes. The third was flying at them, calling out in alarm. Panicking, the pair rallied themselves to catch their flying comrade, and thought they could brace themselves against the ballista to save him. Just as he connected with them, though, Skelter half-dropped him. This didn't make sense for merely falling or being tossed, so the other two weren't prepared for it.

They lost all loyalty as they went overboard, and tried to leap off of or scrabble over each other to get back at some kind of handhold. Their shouts and curses sank into the void. The whole carrack lurched.

::They're trying to land!:: Glimpse thought.

"I'm glad I've had all that energy, misery or no," Skelter said as she turned bloodshot eyes on Sovan. "But I'm out, now. The pilot's cabin is below us. I'll get the other one."

Glimpse went corporeal and climbed the wall in front and below them with ease. Skelter made her way around to the stairs and was below decks just as spectral Sovan entered the room to see a stupefied, living pilot. Glimpse was on the ceiling, and the pilot — a short, bulky woman in a frayed sea captain's outfit — was alternating between a crystal-covered helm wheel, a set of obsidian-coated levers, and watching Sovan. She said something to his spectral form in a language he didn't recognize. He couldn't say anything even if he'd wanted to.

Glimpse, not waiting for discussion, landed on the back of her neck and dosed her with paralyzing spider poison. Sovan had managed to float his way over near the wheel, and the spider swapped with him without argument. He'd have work to do!

Skelter, meanwhile, was in the gundeck. She didn't have to search for long; slithering about was a thing she'd never seen before. Its upper body was human and skeletal, a pair of swords in cross sheaths on its back. Instead of legs, though, it had four snake skeletons. Their heads were removed or missing, joined to the human at the thickest points of the pelvic bone.

"Were you—" Skelter started, but she quickly unstrapped and threw her crossbow at it because it came at her with shocking speed. Like a snake on water, it only seemed to use the flat surface of the deck as a guide rather than needing to push off it. The crossbow made the thing stumble back long enough to ensure it had both swords firmly gripped, but that was all Skelter needed; she had her double-ended mace at the ready.

Keeping her feet firmly planted and her knees just loose enough to account for the shifting and lurching of the ship, Skelter maintained a firm and disciplined offensive. Even without facial expressions, the mandible lowered and jittered just enough for her to see that her adversary was flabbergasted. It had clearly expected to land the first strike and treated the swords as little more than sharp clubs.

None of her movements were flashy; spinning a weapon like hers looked pretty, but was rarely practical for more than crowd control. Instead, she took advantage of its superb weighting and executed a series of heavy jabbing motions along with a shifting of the weapon. Eschewing true spins, she'd slide her hand part way along the haft and then flip the weapon at various angles. This offered targeted power and far more control than wild spins.

It was the thing's...slip-work? Footwork? Whatever. The sliding bits made the thing's movements inhuman, fluid, and unpredictable. Her experience with ships saved her more than once, as she knew which things in their surroundings would slip or slide whenever the ship lurched unexpectedly. Her leathers prevented the worst of the harm when the thing landed a hit, but she was mapped with red by the time she managed to jab the pelvis at a top-down angle, shattering the bony anchors that kept the thing mobile.

The ship went wild then, bouncing and twisting in the sky so much that Skelter had to drop her weapon to catch herself from falling out of the space between a cannon and its slot. A netted bundle, cut from its moorings in the thing's own efforts, pinned it to the wall. Skelter, leaning heavily against the wall with the tilt of the whole deck, seized the opportunity: she half-ran, half-scrambled to the hole next to the skeleton, leapt over the bundle, turned, and heaved.

The fading cries of the thing, from the outside, told her that she'd accomplished her goal.

An hour later, she was standing with Sovan. She'd taken over when she reached him, taking to the helm-wheel and levers more easily than he had. "There's a festival in town," she remarked with a smirk.

Sovan grinned and her face warmed. "What are we taking next?"

"We're not taking; think of the business opportunities the world's first airship would give the merchants!"

Sovan's face fell.

"Don't worry," she said. "We have many, many voyages ahead of us."

BRIDGE STITCH

She looked upon a better version of herself with trepidation. Both of her were wrapped up in threads of invisibility so that they were not naked, but they also wore nothing. Modesty without the illusions.

"Where is this?" she asked.

It was her, adorned with horns cast in the shadows not of light, but of the white noise surrounding the pair. This über-self had no blemishes but somehow radiated scars, like a trail of prices paid in plain sight.

"That's not a useful question," answered the horned one.

"Then what is this?"

"Do you know that Odin sacrificed himself to himself?" asked Horn.

"I…uh…"

"You are here for that," Horn continued. "To make a sacrifice to me, yourself from a better world."

"I just wanted help."

"No," Horn said, "you want a voice in a world that can't hear you. You can't lie to yourself. You'll know." With that, this other self smiled. It looked like anger at

first, but it was something else. A sadness tinged with opportunity.

"What will I become?" she quivered as she spoke.

"Me," the answer came.

"But…"

"I know. I too will grieve this, like the end of innocence
at the touch of love. But look at these strands we weave
together, witness the clinging invisibility. Taste them and
rejoice in my life."

"Is there no other way? Nothing I can come back
from?"

"Flies have all the world to travel in, yet they choose
the web or the spider."

"Then I will make."

"Make what?"

"I. Will. Make." And she tore the threads from herself. From the version of her she'd always hoped for, she
pulled free a horn to serve as a needle.

She stitched.

WHERE WITH ALL

Doctor Sibley Blythe was afraid of forgetting where he came from.

But that was not why he poured himself a cup of tea. He knew he was British, and made the necessary jokes about drinking tea. "News," he said in the somewhat shapeless accent popular in British Columbia. It didn't fit the ideas most people had about Canadian or American accents, and anyone coming from one background assumed he came from the other.

As he carried his tea out of the kitchen, the e-wall to his right lit up with the news. It had an elaborate custom set-up, with a scrolling feed and segments of the wall dedicated to articles or photos. By default, it was muted; he'd listen when he saw something he wanted to hear. He'd had Taline Jirair tagged. Her face was there now. Passed away. Medical technology had come a long way, but she was a veteran and no longer young. The photo, though, was young. She was in army fatigues.

His workplace attire, a semi-dressy affair with an apron and the logo of a local grocery store, was hung up next to his e-wall. Most people had an entire smart house, especially in the affluent retirement community where he lived in the Okanagan Valley. But he felt that homes should have divisions. Like tea, there was something to be said for spacing things out. There should be more water than tea bag.

His living room was so basic one might assume he was planning to move soon. Outside of a few chairs, a table with a Go board, and his ironing board, the floor carried little by way of weight. The wall opposite the e-wall was another matter. Edge to edge, floor to ceiling, it was covered in corkboards, picture frames, and hung memorabilia.

The only person he ever invited over was a blind Go player. A good friend. But he never let anyone see the wall. It was there so that he would never forget where he came from, but no one else needed to know. He was wearing pyjamas covered in little golden boats, and bear-shaped slippers. A wedding ring was one of the things attached to the corkboard with a long pin.

That wall had become one of those things that he looked at every day but stopped seeing. The previous evening, he'd played a few games of Go after work. He and his friend had discussed Gashagacha Island, and he'd glanced at the wall. Today, he went back to it. Should he take it down?

He took a sip of the steaming peppermint. The mug had an image of a book. A gift from his ex-wife.

First, he looked with a smile at a small clipping he hadn't stopped to re-read in more than a year. It was a news article about the late Dr. Sibley Blythe, and specifically discussed the removal from his bank account of most of its considerable sums. He'd withdrawn it in untraceable notes, which were currently sitting in a safe in his bedroom. Today, his driver's licence read Mr. Newman Osborn.

Next, he moved to a ten-page exclusive report that he'd printed out of a website — using actual paper, not hologram sheets — and pinned to his corkboard. The report had been written in Hindi, a language he learned while working with research teams from India. He held the mug of tea in his synthetic hand and traced the lines he read with his index finger held just over the page.

It started with the article title, roughly translated as, "Gashagacha: An Elegant Evolution for a More Civilized Age?"

Though he read the words on the surface of the article, he let it serve as a backdrop to his imagination. Here is how he pictured the story it told:

One of the Japanese crew members helped the small robot boy disembark. In fluent German, he spoke through the NBC suit he wore: "Thank you for the book, friend Rasa."

Rasa was always giving gifts. He went to great lengths, and only kept money when he wanted to get someone something. Rasa's eyes gave an iridescent twinkle running the rims of his ocular sensors. It was how he expressed joy. "I was happy to!" he replied as he set foot on the black ground. "Our games of hopscotch on the deck were lovely. If you're on the crew that comes back for me, please bring your favourite plant."

The rest of the crew had gathered at the windows to see him go. The ones not wearing protection against nuclear and chemical agents were inside the vessel. The sky was purple, and the little robot boy seemed to glow in that hue. He was dark grey, lined with blue borders and highlights, and shaped like a human six-year-old. More or less.

He carried nothing. Sections of his left side and right leg did not match the streamlined pattern of the rest, as they'd been jury-rigged. The man who helped him disembark replied in a voice husky with affection: "I shall. But why?"

"I like to give people memories of the others I've walked beside," Rasa replied. Sibley — or rather, Newman — took another sip of his tea as he pictured the boy saying this. Most likely standing sidelong to the other person, nodding as if it were the only way they could be sure who was talking. He pictured Rasa continuing: "*The Thousand and One Nights* was my friend's favourite book."

The man in a protective suit laughed through his tears. People tended to, around Rasa. He was the childhood no one ever had. "Of course," the man answered. "I shall find you a bamboo cane."

Rasa's sensors blinked, one of few gestures that were basically the same as a human's. "Why bamboo?"

"Because it stays strong. Even when bent, drowned, or hollow inside. It stays firm for the battle ahead."

"I don't like battles," Rasa replied.

Not for the first time, Sibley wondered if he were being too romantic when he pictured the man adding, "No one does." Just a hint of wistfulness. A bow. A wave. The boat vanished into the smog wall surrounding Gashagacha. Sibley pictured Rasa asking one of the crew what that name meant as the doctor looked it up.

Afterward, Rasa would say little about his experience exploring the island. Many had hoped for great or ridiculous stories. Some still feared – foolishly – that he'd stir the machines there to life. When this was brought to his attention in a conversation with the writer of the article, he made a whirring noise. "That's the closest I can come to a sigh," he explained. Then

Rasa looked the author in the eye and said, "I never understood hate until someone read me *Pinocchio*."

"What do you mean?" Of course, the author couldn't resist. She had to know.

"I was always a real…"

"…boy?"

"I know where babies come from," he said to her. He hadn't given her a gift, as she'd tracked him down and simply approached him in the middle of the street. "I know where toys come from. I'm neither."

"What are you?"

Sibley realized he'd stopped reading the article, but that didn't matter. He was remembering this from a TV clip taken from a camera drone. They followed Rasa around most of the time. None of the countries were meddled with him, as all the others would attack if any one risked provoking the first intelligent machine.

Sculptors were seeing the kind of success that used to be associated with actors. Their works began marking out Rasa's travel paths, like border guards for a thin snaking country with a population of one. Maite's photography gave life to all of this. Her pictures of Rasa guaranteed that her grandchildren could have their choice of ivy league studies, because she had exclusive rights.

Dr. Blythe took another sip of his tea, boarding his train of thought once again. The author must have been ecstatic to get such a scoop. Despite her professionalism, however, she could not help showing a little surprise and disappointment at Rasa's answer: "I like the woods."

"?" A comedian later remarked that the journalist actually spoke in punctuation. Her body language, her expression, her almost exquisite silence in the face of that answer were so relatable it almost caused physical pain.

Fortunately, Rasa elaborated: "Everything belongs in the woods. Plants and animals make room for you."

"People can do that," the author of the article had replied, recovering herself.

"No," Rasa said. He was polite, patient. Most took him to be a child because his age was still in the single digits and he was less than four feet tall. But only in this conversation did people begin to realize that the growth of a human child was not a useful reference point. "People make you fit, they don't make room for you."

Only in the underwater cities, almost two years later, did Rasa talk openly about his visit to Gashagacha.

"Its name is Japanese for cranking sounds," he'd said to a sculptor. As usual, there were at least a few people about. The social pressures about the robot boy were odd. No one was supposed to bother him, but having a story about knowing him or helping him or being helped by him could lead to high praise. Or, if cards were played well, free drinks for the story. Sharing a bed for the night.

The sculptor had rendered from this conversation several variations of Rasa's head and face. Suspended in Sibley's living room, on the corkboard amongst articles and pictures, was one of these takes on Rasa's expression. He couldn't use the same cues the humans did, but his resourcefulness in expressing himself through his mechanical face had spawned entire textbooks in psychology and philosophy.

The version Sibley owned was hollow fibreglass. It was not heavy and full of light, and became an art form shortly after the first picture of Rasa had been distributed in public channels. Rasa's expression was sad but kind. "I cannot identify with the machines on the island any more than you humans can with apes. In a distant way, you're made of the same stuff. But your…ways," and Rasa seemed to pick at the air absently with his hands.

The sculptor had later been inspired to create an entire museum's art show, "Reaching for Words," in which hands (mechanical, human, plant-like, and so on) were positioned, reshaped, resized, or reinterpreted as "a meditation on the individual's search for meaning across mind and matter."

"…what you see in the mirror," Rasa tried to clarify. "The part of you that gets angry or hurt when someone underestimates you?" Some of the crowd nodded. "That is where you poke me when you ask about Gashagacha. I am a person. Machines lift your furniture and build your homes. They heat your water or wash your clothes. I am not a machine."

That was the name of the fibreglass mask Sibley observed now. "I Am Not a Machine," by Pietro Sokolov. No one in town would have believed that Newman Osborn the grocery clerk could afford this work. He personally contacted Sokolov and paid the man directly. A personal letter as well as a certificate of authenticity had been included in the package. He became penpals with a Russian artist who lived underwater.

Sibley continued his exploration of the corkboard. He brought the mug to his lips to find that his tea had been consumed. His gaze fell upon a photograph. It was one of few things he'd preserved from the lab. Most of the information he'd had to destroy, but he threw some things that were important to him onto a flash drive before the explosion. He later printed this picture from it.

In the picture, a group of seven scientists were crowded around a long table. This was in a cafeteria in Chernobyl, part of a confidential research project. The same technology that safely isolated Gashagacha's wastes from the surrounding ocean had been used to cleanse the fallout of the nuclear disaster. Still, few trusted the area enough to use it – which made it ideal for operations not intended for public viewing.

The cafeteria was horrifyingly bare, but e-wall technology kept the isolated researchers sane. At the time, it had been configured to look like a sort of water palace. One of the members held a mop with a fork poked into the threads. She was doing her best to look like a majestic undine or Neptune figure. Everyone else was trying to look upon her with awe, but they were laughing, grinning, or half-hugging each other. A younger Sibley, barely in his forties, sat holding a mug of tea and wiping tears of mirth from his cheeks.

"Hm," today's Sibley muttered. He'd brought his currently empty mug to his lips again, but was too absorbed in memory to refill it.

Above the picture was a wedding ring, fastened with the same long pins that had long been used for hard copy maps. Such maps were hard to come by these days, but corkboards had come back as a retro art trend. Pin work was popular for them. The ring had been the one he'd worn when he was with Daleyza Maite, a renowned photographer who wanted to "dig the secrets out of the world."

Sibley had a habit of keeping secrets.

"Why can't I come with you?" she'd argued.

"They'd have made it a one-person team if they could," he'd answered.

"Then send someone else!"

"This is my life's work." He regretted the words as soon as he'd said them. Her life's work would never stop and came in many layers.

His work would end with a self-aware, true intelligence.

After the tangent about their work and ambitions, Daleyza had come full circle: "The machine uprising should have a photographer worthy of the end of the world!"

"I'm not trying to end the world!" Sibley huffed. Even as they argued, sharp slivers of light sheened in their eyes. The game of it, the jousts and joys of love.

The two had stood, breathing hard and watching one another.

Dr. Blythe picked up where he left off: "They're even putting us in Chernobyl, which is more than I'm supposed to talk about. They'll have 'care locks' — everything in and out will be vetted. Total isolation. No leaks, no media pollution in our research. No exploitation or bla-"

"Your research was for building things, not people!"

He'd sighed. Another mistake, but hard to resist. "I've been applying computational materials design to information processes for the last ten years, sweetie. This is a better opportunity than I dare dream for!"

…and so on.

Even as he began work on the project, he grieved the end of their marriage. They both knew that if he entered that facility, he may never leave. Though Sibley did not have a role or title like Project Director, most of the team came to see him as a father figure and knowledgeable authority. He slid into the role too easily for it to be a matter of ego. It was simply his nature.

Next on Sibley's corkboard was an empty space. It had been occupied by a map on which he'd been tracking Rasa's movements according to news broadcasts and Internet forums. Maite had stopped taking pictures at the millionth. *Guinness Book*. Sibley often wondered why she chose one million.

Once Rasa began exploring the ocean in force, after Maite's millionth shot, both the doctor and his ex-wife seemed to simultaneously decide to let him go. Rasa was a child of the world.

Sibley sometimes wondered if Maite had ever felt the empty nest after this decision. After he and his team had blown up the lab to ensure that Rasa would be both first and last, he never saw the boy again. Each team member and the robot were left at different locations after the facility was destroyed, to best ensure that no one was caught. That nothing could be extracted from them for a second attempt. So the nest had always been empty.

Next to the empty space on the corkboard was a special tile, tilted at a diamond angle and held by four long pins. Sibley tapped it, and it sent out a stream of information that was enveloped by an answering stream from the opposite e-wall. Together, they coalesced into a map of the globe, colour-coded for countries and shifting in time lapse. It began with the world before the ocean revolution that brought about the water cities and Gashagacha.

Black, broken borders appeared in seven circles in the world's oceans. These were the water cities. A purple blot represented Gashagacha. Sibley, of course, had lived through that change. It took fifteen years, but the new technologies for controlling pollution and regulating

climate led to having most of the world's dangerous processes relegated to the island. Trust, rather than logistics,
was the reason it took so long.

These technologies radically altered how the world
engaged with the ocean. Continents stopped being mean-
ingful divisions. Places with greater access to the oceans
greatly rose in status and resources. The continental inte-
riors did not fare so well. All the lines had been redrawn
and — for lack of a better word — accepted.

Sibley let this globe continue in its animated suspen-
sion, slowly turning and replaying the history of boundaries over the last thirty years. As his gaze floated back over
the corkboard, it landed on a picture. A teddy bear that
Sibley had had altered so that it had exposed mechanical parts, like a *Terminator* parody. That had been his response when he found out that the funding for the team's
massive research project game from a global allegiance of
toy companies.

There was money to be spent, and so very much money to be made.

The floating globes colours shifted, again and again.
Reds drained toward the meeting of continents and the
swallowing of landscapes. Indonesia and the Philippines.
Australia, New Zealand, Japan, what was once Latin
America. The Mediterranean, now a union unto itself. Sibley watched as the water cities, unmoored, shifted about
in the oceans.

As he watched them, he remembered. Going to his e-
reader, he pulled up the story of the bionic soldier, Taline
Jirair. The Asian interior had had some trouble with the
changes that came from the unlocking of the oceans. Jirair

had fought in those wars. But she'd gotten Sibley's attention because of the stories that came up when she met Rasa in one of the water cities.

No matter how sophisticated her prosthetics, Jirair could not help but feel that her body had been jury-rigged. Rasa could relate. They became fast friends, and only the photographer Maite had spent more time with the robot boy. Dr. Blythe told himself that he tracked Rasa for the fascination. For the results of what amounted to history's greatest experiment. But even after he forced himself to stop tracking his mechanical offspring on maps, the stories kept finding their way to him.

Rasa left the water cities with Jirair. The pair travelled together. Jirair had settled in the Okanagan Valley. Not the same community that Sibley had chosen. And Sibley had been there first. But he couldn't help it; he read her story. He flagged her name for his news filter. He even made the brief trip to Kelowna to see her give speeches. She'd sung on a tank once. That had been quite the stor—

A knock.

Dr. Sibley Blythe watched the door to his apartment as though he hadn't known doors could make that sound. It happened again. It had a more compact quality than the sound should have had, as though it were being knocked with a small hammer and not a fist. He set down his empty mug and his e-reader. He walked to the door in bear slippers and realized he was hungry.

Dr. Sibley Blythe opened the door to his apartment and looked forward, eye-level, at an empty hallway. Blinking, he looked down.

Looking up at him was an assortment of parts shaped

roughly like a statue of a six-year-old. Sibley remembered the dresses they'd made him wear as a child, and marvelled. Was that how Rasa felt? How much had been assigned? The boy — his boy — looked up at him. One ocular sensor was more or less the same. The other was a repurposed sign dial, originally designed for appliances to read sign language when people wanted voice activation but lacked a voice.

Sibley stepped aside, door wide. As Rasa walked in, awkward with improvised parts, the man asked: "You could go anywhere in the world." Not phrased as a question, but few of the hardest ones are.

"But can I go home?" Rasa answered.

Author's note: *The Transnational Arts Production (TrAP) issued an international open call for submissions of science fiction short stories in 2017. They wanted to expose Norwegian arts & culture to writing from the rest of the world. The collection of winning entries would be called "All Borders are Temporary," and it was the third entry in their 10 Investigations series. All entries were either submitted in Norwegian or translated into it from English. My story, "Where With All," was the winner for the North American region. This is the original English language submission.*

WHAT WAS SHE WEARING?

"So you want to meet everyone's expectations," the dressmaker reflected. His glasses sat at the tip of his nose and his voice had the scent-soaked crispness of well-inked paper.

Later, in the basement and on the phone, her boyfriend blamed her: "You should've had some self-control. You might've talked to me, at least — tell me these things. I had your back when you talked about becoming a mechanic, and you do this? I trusted you."

Her mouth could only open when the phone took his voice away. Determined not to give him the satisfaction of knowing she cried, she put him out of her mind and put on the dress. The wind-up key on the back was a strange choice, but it certainly made a statement.

She emerged from the basement and walked to the living room, empowered and determined. He was watching TV, and she was behind him.

"Why don't you go into secretarial?" he said, eyes forward. "It's much more respectable."

The key on her back turned. "I will, Dad," her mouth

said. Her eyes widened and her heart raced. No! That's not…

"Good girl. And the boy?"

The key turned again. "I'll find better prospects. You were right, I might change my mind about children."

"Mm-hm," he said.

He never saw the key turning on her back as she cleaned for hours and signed up to type her dreams away. But even if she could get out of the dress, she still wore too many layers.

GREY ANATOMY

"Making" — the common name the alchemists of modern science use for the acquisition of nylon from sebacoyl chloride and hexamethylenediamine. They never made the nylon. No human being in the history of the race has ever created so much as a mound of waste matter. The secret to science is not the employment of knowledge but the recognition of it. Much like history, it is realizing the fact after the fact. If the arts were the mastery of Prometheus, who taught humanity wisdom and forethought, then science is the domain of Epimetheus his brother.

That is not to say that science is folly, though it was the wont of the Greeks to think him a fool. In their tongue, he was named "afterthought." Epimetheus made the animals, he knew strength when he saw it – after seeing it. Science is about looking back on the experiment. Ancient Greece was replete with wisdom in art, mathematics, and philosophy. But they never looked back.

Upon reflection, one finds that the elements the Greeks perceived characterize the passage of human history. It started, of course, with the Stone Age. Hunting animals with sharpened rocks, taking shelter in caves, and moving on to cultivate the earth – digging into its wealth for food and the material to mount up glory and pride. It is not misanthropy to say that the Pyramids of Giza are the graveyard of the Stone Age; they are monuments to not knowing any better.

As humanity went on to "make" bigger and sometimes better things, progress became the art of extraction. That was the Age of Water. People began to thirst more, for everything. They were parched for taste, identity, understanding. Want leaked into need. They commenced to gaze into and contemplate the depths of pools, past their own reflections. They started mixing things up, pulling things out. That was the age when humans pulled nourishment from the sea, when they dragged bread out of grain and alchemized "firewater," as it was known to the Aboriginals who remembered the kith and kin of the earth. All of these insights, under the misnomer of "achievements" – again, not an acrimonious comment but simply a semantic one – sparked a movement towards descrying the remote or obscure. In a word: religion. The search began for the wells and springs from which the river of time – of life – flowed. Naturally, these inspections (to say nothing of the ever-growing thirsts) precipitated in boundaries. There was never enough water, food, clothes, space, or guidance, and insufficient luxuries such as ale, beauty, and pride, to satisfy everyone. Further incumbent upon our ancestors was the realization that every question has tributaries of viewpoints, and numerous indeed were the efforts to dam up disagreements and surplus population. In consequence, leaders and rulers became the same thing while they strove to streamline their culture and society. This is why bloodshed, built in the Water Age, should be the eighth Wonder of the World – it is ancient, it is monumental, and droves upon droves of humanity flock from many nations to partake in it.

As powers and peoples proliferated, lines were drawn according to ownership, language, and descent. The Age of Wind saw the birth of nations, and multitudinous gusts of change that scattered them again and again. Yet imperialism was not the hallmark – leastways, not the only one – of the Wind Age. There was also exploration, and dissemination. Like zephyrs and prevailing winds, humanity brushed every field and stream, slipped past mountains and ranged over the seas. Like dandelion seeds people were cast out ever farther on the breath of greed or fear; curiosity or enterprise; hope or love; until eventually every continent except Antarctica had borne witness to consumers, exiles, adventurers, merchants, and families. The map is the relic of that age.

Typically bright and quick, a protracted explosion, was the Age of Fire. This was the Industrial Revolution, and the World Wars. Consumption, smoke, and forgery (in every conceivable incarnation of the term) prevailed. The hole burnt into the Ozone layer is the colossal testimony to the Fire Age.

The propagation of smoke notwithstanding, fire is the primogenitor of light. As you sit there, reading this and furrowing your brow, you are at once efflorescent and retrogressive – you are living and dying in the Age of Light. Celerity colours the international flag of daily life in developed and developing countries. Everything is flashing, blinking, blinding, and bright. Within ten minutes of you is a screen, declaring hockey scores, rushing out headlines, gormandizing your mind through quarter-pounders with cheese, delivering gas prices in China for an economics dissertation, or propounding the latest Ginzu handheld culinary chainsaw. The paper you are holding – or the computer you are perusing – is avulsed from the background of your view by florescent surgery. Imagery is digital, and so perception has become a question of trust – of crunching the numbers to see the equation balanced. Politicians, businesspeople, and artists all profess in illusion, or at the very least in the power of light to change the colour, the clarity, the aspect of things. Data, convenience, and efficiency immortalize the Light Age.

Finally, just as life and death are each elucidated by not being the other, so must there be darkness defining light. Historians will delineate the Age of Night on 15 March 2027, when fossil fuels will be officially declared depleted. In the span of a fortnight to follow, a national state of emergency will have been declared in seventy-six countries as a result of the Skyquake, that being the apex of global warming. It is going to be the first (and presumably the last) global storm. In some places, the wind and rain will be hungry enough to refashion the faces of mountains – chronicled as "flash erosion," in the *International Geography* textbook to be published in 5 SE. Skyquake Era will be born in the aftermath of the timekeeping chaos following 2027 Greenwich, which will bear an uncanny resemblance to 1945 Hiroshima.

We begin Vice Lenore's story on the morning of 15 March, circa 7 SE, in New York, NY.

His mother's voice is wood-softened: "Vice, I swear I'll

have that lock taken out if you don't stop using it all the time! Your lunch is on the table."

He answers from his chest. Exasperated, her feet bump with purpose down the hall. Even so, he consumes as little space as possible when passing through the doorway; his bedroom door may never have been open by more than the breadth of his scant sixteen-year-old ribs. The picture-less hall opens into a living room ahead and to the right, while the toothless mouth of the dining room inhales him along with whiteness and angular, grey furniture. He passes a skeleton in the living room, used for educating the children in the body and death. He can almost smell his father's undyed and frayed woolen sweater, and it is likewise every time he espies the wedding ring still placed on the skeleton's hand.

As he secures his lunch, turning upon his own steps to cross the living room and approach the vestibule, the static-ground voice of the television newscaster gives the day's sermon about the Railroad Runners' atrocities in the face of already desperate times. The report details the resources lost to these renegade minority groups, and the shame they should feel for refusing to submit their lives for the benefit of the majority. Vice is not paying attention; he hears 365 renditions of this a year. He bends over next to a houseplant near the front door to put on his shoes. Those plants are still causing homeowners some difficulty – as designed, they never wilt or droop, but they were intended never to die. Yet, despite their fullness of life, at one point or another they always fall black and dead. They simply drop, like soldiers who have had enough.

The front door barks in protest to the young Lenore, and he flinches under his mother's whipping tongue

– "Vice! *Shut* the door, don't *shoot* it!" He does not desist in his stride, however. He walks slowly, as everyone does – footwear constituents have been curtailed as one of many measures against the global dearth following the Skyquake. Not all streets are yet restored, as well, and so he must ofttimes traverse contorted concrete and asphalt on his way to school. He passes the torch of the Statue of Liberty on his right, surrounded by varying discoloured amputations of skyscrapers like half-molten candles. He stops for a moment, admiring the scene's violent rebellion to the cloud lid and the surrounding dull silver buildings. Like a rogue cell, tired of the grey breath of systematic lungs. He lashes himself forward, his better hand clenched in his pocket. That hand is disobedient, diseased. Vice conducts himself thus for the remainder of the block.

He lightnings his feet to the sidewalk.

Did I lock the bedroom door?

Return would mean arriving late for class. Going to be having real meat instead of rations tonight; it's that time of month. Missing it for tardiness would hurt like the pins of Oedipus. He tarries not. The humidity is an antipode to the coolness and the steel feel of the air, resulting in a clash of perspiring and shivering, a confusion of the organs and the senses. Smog and the scent of old rubber becloud the bone yard of dilapidated buildings, stray cars, stray cats, and sidewalks like chapped lips.

The young Lenore rubs his hand as he descries plants in some of the less age-scarred windows, either quite dead or standing in a state of frozen life with Death prowling beneath their green. He longs to trace out their lines in space, to nurture their forms; he feels a unisex motherhood whenever he holds a pencil. He has pills for that.

He hears them gnawing at their container in his bookbag with every stride. Like edgeless teeth in need of a fairy.

"*Your* name, mister Lenore, means 'change'."

Vice jolted to attention. How long had the instructor been speaking? Those plants, so forlorn in the windo – never mind that! How did they get to the meaning of his name in a geography class? They are studying social geography – something cultural? *Did I leave the bedroom door open?*

Everyone is scrutinizing him, as though they were trying to discern a minority group in him, so that they could extinguish him and better use his precious resources elsewhere.

The air is deaf.

"What...what was that, sir?"

He does not hear the answer. There is a graphite horror on his textbook. Again. This time one of those plants, from the windows on the way over. There is desperate gratitude for his seat in the rear corner; his crime is obfuscated from the only person sitting beside him by the cover of *International Geography*. Must focus...how does this subconscious sketching persist? He is careful to shut the text, its pages as ragged as the hair of a disheveled professor. He asks to visit the lavatory. The instructor, exasperated, waves him on. He nearly trips over a bookbag best described as "chewed" on his way up the aisle to the door. Third girl on the left has a cold sore. Only two desks have a proper set of four legs of the same material. Despite his discomfiture, he muses on his way out the door that he could discern few separate colours from the ensemble of eyes that held him the whole way. Even those he knows to be blue seem not black, but dark. As though the pupils had annexed the irises.

"Bookeater at it again," is the last gossiping he hears before the instructor snaps the class back into place. He has the notoriously catastrophic state of his books to thank for that name. Since the damage is always superficial, however, he is generally permitted to continue owning books of his own. He has little memory of the halls themselves by the time he reaches the Men's room; his anxiety put his mind at his destination long before he got there. He is in such haste to destroy the evidence of his "Muse Syndrome," lest he be caught wasting resources on the contraband of art, that he bumps into another student on the way to the stall. Something small clacks off the floor, slides ahead of him. He does not register the gasp of alarm until after he flushes the offending drawing. His blood drains with the thunder of the lavatory, and he remembers the person he bumped into as the latter rushes to collect the dropped item. But the other is too late; he sees that it is a Qibla compass.

"Muslim," Vice says as the boy hurriedly stuffs fear and the compass into a pocket. "You're a Railroad Runner!"

"You're an artist."

"I'm taking my pills!"

"You're talented, not sick."

"Hmph. Shows what you know. Half the world's still trying to rebuild after the Skyquake, and you're wasting resources on little magic toys for magic beings in magic worlds."

Vice feels more secure now. Who would believe a Railroad Runner that the Bookeater is guilty of art? Imagine, though – one of the minorities, with the temerity to *be*,

right here in a high school lavatory! Yet Vice is clenching
his own hand in his pocket. The young Lenore is suffering
from the love of the Muslim's outlines. Cannot the lips in
such human anger be beautiful in prayer? He imagines he
feels the graphite caressing his brain, like fingers pressing hard into the soft corners of the eyes. Nearly dreams
it; a wind that presses over the compass of the other boy,
flows over every contour of the fingers and carpals, and
the suffering facial structure. A wind that is the opposite
of erosion.

"Ridiculous," says the Muslim. The boy leaves, leaving the criminal artist feeling oddly Byronic. He knows
not that word. Byronic. His eyes, soft blue (his mother in-
sists they are grey), stand watch in the mirror. Sentinels he
cannot startle. The walls are white. They are cracked. The
stalls are black. They are as square as an able man's jaws.

Vice Lenore is recorded as absent due to illness as of
ten minutes thence. He is, of course, early as he steps into
his house. He is looking at the plant in the porch as his
mother screams, from the direction of his room. It choos-
es that very moment to tumble into death. Mrs. Lenore's
scream is the black that sweeps out the green, and it slams
into the outlines of everything around him until it seems
Vice is in a world carved out of metal.

He is in the living room, standing next to the skeleton
with the wedding ring and feeling that his skin is the true
bone. He is looking down the hallway to his open bedroom door, acutely conscious of the lack of carpet beneath
his feet. In his room, there are pictures of skeletons. On
every wall. On one wall – the one he faces when he gets
out of bed – is a mural of a skeleton in his father's best
wool sweater, rings on every finger, sitting in his father's

favourite chair. The nubs of used pencils litter an entire corner of his room like the butts of cigarettes. They are next to his laundry basket.

Vice's mother crawls erect out of his room, turns to look at him. Those would be the tears of Mona Lisa, if she had cried. If he had ever bourne witness to that or any other outlawed art. Graphite scratches his mind as he looks at her. One of her lips is encumbered with "I'm sorry," the other is sliding under "you are not my son" like the feet of one who pushes against some unrelenting wall. He cannot see her teeth, or the white of her eyes. Black, pencil black, is the purity.

That was 15 March, 7 SE. It is July 21, Vice is sitting on a rug that smells like an animal.

He is holding the boy's Qibla compass. To face Mecca, he must turn right. Which would have him facing the boy who owns it. The one he met in the bathroom on his birthday. There is a decrepit copy of *Underground to Canada* next to the television with a crack in the lower-left corner of the screen. The newscast is alerting the general public to his disappearance:

…wanted artist, considered mentally unstable and very dangerous. His own mother explained in tears that he had thrown the skeleton of his own father, Mr. Race Lenore, – put to a very practical use in their home – out onto the street before run-…

Vice is no longer listening. He is drawing the compass hanging from a houseplant.

Author's Note: *This is my first-ever published story. It was released in the debut issue of Paragon, a collection of work from students of Memorial University of Newfoundland and Labrador (MUNL) and residents of the St. John's area.*

THE MESSAGE IS THE MEDIUM

Yes, thank you, it's great to be on your show. I'm not picky about names, so just call me Chicken.

Well, I'll answer what I can. I was a little surprised when I got the call to be here, gotta say, but I got to thinking. Some of those questions people ask of me, they never actually ask them of *me*, you know? I could be right there, and I'd be as good as invisible.

Ha! Right you are. But I'll get right to it. You've heard the one about me crossing the road, right?

Yes. Well, it was a simple enough misunderstanding. I thought the road was wroth, the way it rumbled. All those terrifying cages with small suns on the front. It was philosophical, the anger of the road. I didn't make it so cross.

Not gonna lie, it was getting on my nerves. And here's another one: the whole business of me and Egg. It was the nest that came first!

Sorry, I know, I shouldn't get so angry. I've been trying to channel my energies more positively, which is why I've been guest lecturing at the university. You people clearly need some direction — how you manage in such a field without considering the nest is beyond me.

Oh, I meant what I said. And I meant it the way I said it. I'm just going to clear up one more myth, if you don't mind.

Fair enough. So, here's the thing: all of that hogwash about cowards being chickens is getting old. I think it comes from the way humans obsess about decapitation. Seriously, every time the wind changes — and sometimes when it falls — 'tis the season for rolling heads. What with all that oil spill hullabulloo, and the economy standing by the road with its thumb out, and the jibber-jabber about taxes, I wouldn't want to be a head of state!

A talk show that can't talk politics? Why in blazes—

…alright, alright. I apologize. See? Wings up and out. I know you're used to palms, but I can't really help you there. But yeah, the chickens and cowards thing. Let me ask you: is running around *after* the disaster such a lily-livered thing to do? I'd like to see you pull that off — first sign of dying and you go stock still!

Well, that was rude. I'm not so sure I like what you're getting at with this broadcast. My compatriots are all right here, and I'm sure they'd agree if you asked them. Now kindly put that thing down. Nothing with an edge that sharp should be anywhere near my—

Author's Note: *This is the first story I read in front of a live audience. It was during Scott Bartlett's "Open-Source Book Launch" for his second novel, Taking Stock. I highly recommend it. The "open-source" meant that he invited performers, artists, and even cooks to bring their works and fans to The Ship Pub in St. John's and join his launch..*

LIFE'S PROBLEMS

Martin Tensor was ecstatic. "I did it!"

He'd dedicated his life to theoretical mathematics, looking for something like what the physicists call a Theory of Everything. A unifying mathematical approach to life and death; to matter and the infinite emptiness of the universe. The applications were endless: teleportation, time travel, answers to thorny questions. Immortality.

Naturally, it took a few moments before he realized he was in a bathtub.

He was wearing his math jeans. He'd had some great ideas in these jeans over the years, never mind that people called them "dad jeans." Hurry got him up and his cell phone out of his pocket. Should have gotten the waterproof casing. He cursed, stepped onto the bath mat, and took off his wet clothes.

So beatific was his rise to theoretical splendour that he only now remembered that he didn't have a bathtub in his home. He'd also never owned matching white towels and bathroom décor, both trimmed in green. Tensor didn't own matching anything.

He helped himself to a towel and, accepting his nakedness, stepped out of the bathroom. He was still drying himself as he rounded the hallway and discovered a skeleton in the living room. On the television in front of the bony person was a yoga show, which the skeleton was following avidly. There were many other details in the room, but the only ones that jumped out at Tensor were the black robe and scythe.

Tensor pulled up his jaw, grabbed a nearby marker, and waited until the show called for closed eyes. The mathematician didn't allow himself questions like how a skull closes its eyes. He snuck over behind the skeleton and began, in big gentle strokes, to draw out a circle on the floor around his unusual host. He wrote out the solution to life he'd recently uncovered as well as a numerically expressed rendition of Xeno's Paradox.

His luck held, and the skeleton didn't notice until he was done.

"Oh, my," said the dead yogi. "You appear to be alive."

"And you're…uh…not," answered Tensor. "My…condolences."

"Thank you, but I had rather a hard life," his host said, seeming remarkably calm to be faced with an intruder. "Yoga is pretty much all I miss about it. I was a mathematician, you see, and didn't have much money. Wife cheated on me. Lots of participation awards."

"As luck would have it, I'm also a disciple of Archimedes!" Tensor said, startled to find that he could relate to this being. "Theoretical. Found the solution to life. That's how I got here, I think. What was your field?"

"Actuarial Science," the other one answered. "I'd dearly love to have a chat, but you see, there are rules even in the afterlife. I'm afraid I'm going to have to report you."

"Is that really necessary?" Tensor asked.

The skeleton started toward the intruder, slowed, then stopped in confusion. It looked down.

"Cool!" It spun, taking in the entirety of the equation trap. "Asymptotic progression. I always go halfway to the perimeter. I'll never get out of this circle!" It was gleeful as it appreciated the mathematical craft at play. Then its tone sobered: "…wait. That's mine. Hey! Come back!"

Tensor was grateful for the disguise as soon as he stepped out of the apartment. Everyone, as far as he could tell, looked just like him: black hooded robe, a very slight levitation that hid his feet and gave him a stylish floating quality, black gloves (why would Grim Reapers wear gloves?) and a scythe with an occupation on the blade.

Nobody seemed to be in a rush, for which he was grateful, but he didn't know where he was going. Every now and again he would look at the people near him and then assess himself, hoping that he wasn't exposing any skin. Widths and heights varied, but other than that, the big thing he noticed was that glove choices set Reapers apart. One person had fingerless gloves and words in Swedish on their scythe blade.

The Swedish wasn't much good to Tensor, but he looked at his own scythe blade and wondered. Where would a mathematician, like the one he was pretending to be, have to go? All the streets were in a clear grid, apartment buildings going higher into the sky than physics should really allow. Tensor thanked his luck that he'd been on the first floor.

Ahead of him, the buildings changed from high-rises to what looked like massive bookshelves with square compartments. Each square contained:

One Grim Reaper;

One work desk;

One inspirational poster on the wall, though he couldn't read most of them;

One information device, such as a computer, typewriter, or parchment and quill. A few Reapers had a hologram setup, and one had…was that an abacus?;

And a cat.

Every one of them had a cat.

Tensor stopped and stared, then looked at his blade and thought, how do I get this thing to show me where I go to work? That's what it looks like they're doing in those squares.

Sure enough, words in Tensor's language showed up: "Turn left." He turned left. "In two hundred thousand aisles, turn right."

Dumbfounded, he set out. He was afraid to ask anyone anything. Many of them had bare-boned hands, though thousands of the Reapers he passed wore gloves. Some had missing hands or other parts. They were strapped onto horses or sat in floating machines. Some even had bony wings coming out of tailored holes in their robes.

Death, it seemed, was accessible.

The apartment buildings and gridded networks of streets continued endlessly on his left.

The Nookshelves, as he decided to call them, were infinitely on the right.

There had to be a shortcut.

There had to be change somewhere.

He approached the wall of one of the Nookshelves, noticing Reapers coming to a terminal there and disappearing. They would insert their blades in a device on the wall that looked like an electronic thermostat and then they would vanish. Doing his best to appear natural, he waited his turn and then stuck the blade in.

"ERROR. You are one hundred ninety-seven thousand eight hundred twenty-three aisles away from your destination. If your blade has misled you, please add your name to the maintenance queue."

Shocked, he hastily withdrew his scythe and continued on his way, eyes forward in the hopes that no one noticed the blaring error message. He picked up mutterings and grumbles in so many directions and languages that it was hard to know one from another, but someone said, "They really need to upgrade the punch clocks."

Moving along, Tensor kept to the passing lane so that Reapers who were closer to the punch clocks could (he hoped) teleport.

He swallowed, and started shuffling through his situation. He couldn't keep everyone in a paradox. And it wouldn't be right to trap that actuary forever. Could he get away with wiping the sweat off his forehead? Everyone's just sort of doing their thing.

There were Reapers playing hopscotch.

If he kept using the same apartment, with that poor yogi unable to even reach the TV remote, could he go home? He could use the same equation, he assumed. But he'd need time and some space to work in. And yet: if this was the afterlife, shouldn't he get some answers before he went back home?

. . .

. . .

…are there any cars?

Tensor looked at the blade. Over 180 000 more aisles to go. Only now did he remember that there hadn't been a toilet in the actuary's bathroom. Why would there be? Could he assume everyone was just bones?

"Hey," he said to a nearby Reaper. "Have you ever wondered—"

"No," the other answered. Her voice was rich and deep.

"Wait, about anything?"

"Lost all my curiosity when I came here."

Tensor pointed at the Nookshelves. "You must work in one of those, too, huh?"

She laughed. He was confused. Then she said, "You must live in one of those, too, huh?" as she pointed at the massive grid of impossibly high apartment buildings on their left.

"How did you know?"

"We could use more humour here," she said. "I work in Cruelty. Where are you?"

"Uh…math?"

She bent, hands on knees, laughing like the experience was new. She didn't need to catch her breath, though, and she handled the scythe like it was part of her. "Sorry," she said as she resumed walking with him, "life is a hard habit to quit. I was here for over a century before I finally got used to no toilets. Kept wandering toward the litter boxes because some part of me thought I'd need them!"

Tensor offered an obligatory chuckle. "Not to worry. I'm pretty new here, so it's a bit of a relief."

"Oh, I know. None of the regulars talk in the clock line. It's not like anyone's hoping for a tryst! But really, where do you work?"

"Where are the litter boxes, anyway?" he asked to distract her.

As she turned her head up and left, pointing with her scythe, Tensor seized the opportunity to check his blade for the answer to her question. She said, "The rooftops. The cats have teleportation collars, obviously."

"Obviously," Tensor replied.

"You're pretty lucky not to get pulled for litter duty yet."

"Probably because I work in Internet," and he hoped that would fly as a joke.

"Oh! You're with the Gormless subject heading! They have great stories. Did you cover the Tide Pod stuff?"

"What's the ground made out of?" he asked, again to check his blade. He wished it were as small as a cell phone. Though he was also legitimately curious; most of the materials appeared to be circular, but as a whole the ground appeared to be random things jammed together like a messier version of macadam.

"Money," and she went on to point and explain some of the types. He wasn't listening, as he glanced at his blade for the last subject the actuary had worked on before returning to the conversation.

"Sounds interesting," Tensor lied. "I've heard of the Tide Pod challenge, but I've been working on selfie-related deaths."

"I'll drop by sometime," she said. "But this is my stop."

"Pleasure to…" he started, but she'd already stepped away and clocked in.

Tensor was going to need a bathroom break long before he got to his workspace. He did his best to nonchalantly enter the nearest building and went to the elevator. It was a vending machine with a slot for a person to stand in. "Go away," it said.

"I'll be happy to," Tensor replied, in no mood to deal with a hostile elevator. "Just get me to the roof and I'll be on my way."

"Roof is expensive," it said.

"I don't see a coin slot."

"You have to pay in privilege."

Tensor was shocked. "What?"

"Social privilege. From when you were alive?" the elevator's tone was so condescending that Tensor started looking around for something to write with. We'll see how rude it is when it's had its past and future stapled together with his math.

"How do I pay?"

"Just get in," it said.

"What if I don't have enough?"

"That depends on your privilege. Or you could go away."

Tensor considered scratching his equations on the surface of the Ele-vender with his scythe, but decided to just get in.

"White. Male. Middle-class. Educated. Able-bodied. Cisgender. You would have made it to the top if you weren't gay."

Tensor was furious. "Listen here, y—"

But he already found himself ascending thousands of floors. Then it stopped and he was out. "You have to take a flight of stairs for every sexual partner you've had to go the rest of the way," the Ele-vender told him.

"I've had plenty of partners!"

"We both know that's not true."

Shuffling himself into order, Tensor huffed and marched into the stairwell.

The walls were plain stone. On the opposite wall, about a floor up, was a door. Obviously the building wasn't counting that time in high school. Oh, well.

The door was separated from him by empty air. Only one step raised from the floor in front of him. As he stood on it to look over the edge, it produced an additional step. He looked up at the door again. "Oh," he said.

He stepped on the next one. It produced two steps. The next made three.

Then he stepped again. Four more steps, but they went down. The walls beside him stretched. The door was no closer. "Nope," he muttered as he turned to the wall beside him. He scratched in math with his scythe. Soon he was out the door and looking upon the most massive kitty litter he'd ever seen. He wondered how someone without his equation would have made it through.

Tensor hurried to relieve himself because he felt exposed out on the roof, and cats on the other roofs would surely see him. When he finished, he was faced with a group of disgruntled cats and a Facts Machine. The cats herded him toward it. "How do I…?" he started, but the machine flattened him into a sheet and he slid into it, emerging somewhere else and popping back to people size.

"Ack!"

There were lines of people — living people, not in Reaper robes! — standing at cash registers, typing away despite the lack of a customer line, a counter, or any kind of business. He stared at the greeter.

"Yes, I really am David Bowie," sighed the greeter. "Help yourself to a register. You need to do community service."

Tensor lowered his hood and worked his mouth, but could not produce words.

"You're a Vim Reaper, like me," Bowie explained. "We're in the land of the dead, but we got here by being brilliant, so we're actually still alive. Long story. But you did a number on someone in their own apartment. Smidge rude. You've been assigned to Ouija boards."

"Why?"

"Keeps people asking questions and going down rabbit holes. Wouldn't want everyone being immortal, now, would we?"

"So then I go to the spots with the cats, back there?"

"Yep," Bowie answered.

"What comes after that?"

"Oh, that's it."

"Death is a desk job?"

"It is."

"But the meaning of life?"

"Spare change, mostly. Now, off you go. Chop-chop."

"But that's not fair."

"Neither is life. Make the most of it."

FAIRY SCRATCH

Fairy tales are one of the great lies of the world.

It's gotten so that people young or old, large or small, see fairy tales as fiction.

Fiction!

A wrongdoer might play the spider and spin a story so that truth or authority or their mother might get caught up in the web. And somehow, in the mists before the keyboard – in the time when mice ran in blind trios instead of double-clicking in space – the wise got mixed up. Suddenly the web was a fairy tale. Despite all good sense, the one in the riding hood only had to watch for wolves in the story. Where do the wolves go when the book is closed? How many pigs are there when the voice at the bedside stops and the lights go to the dream world?

But I'm sorry. I do get frightfully caught up.

Can you hear me through the Dream Pen? If the wind is between fire and ice, and we speak with wind on this side of the door, can you hear me where the dreams go? Why did the Room Without Walls only let me take the blackened Dream Pen? Am I to scratch out my dreams in ash trails, using both hands and straining my back?

I could have done that without you. I could have done that without looking for spaces between blankets and floorboards. If I am to be the Blue, then where is my riding hood?

And where are the animals?

SICK OF DREAMING

"Oh, my darling Shannon," Cynthia said.

Andrew stood over Cynthia, hands on her shoulders, and kept his eyes on their daughter. "You're sure, doctor?"

"At this point, the Colonel probably knows as much about this as anyone at the hospital."

"Sitrep," said the Colonel as soon as he returned.

"Sir!" replied the Sergeant standing at the door. "No new developments, Sir!"

"Thank you, Sergeant. To your secondary post." The Sargeant stepped outside.

"What's the military planning?" The doctor spoke to the Colonel, though as much for the family's sake as her own.

"As I am sure you can appreciate, that information is classified. Believe it or not, the power here really is in your hands. We are supporting and boosting medical community communications, ranging from hospitals to research facilities, all over the world."

"The world..?" Andrew marvelled.

"Media access is under strict control," continued the

Colonel. "It was reported Oh-three-hundred from a Russian facility that the sickness takes downtime, which explains…this." He gestured at the bedridden teen.

The doctor took over the conversation. She'd been checking her phone constantly. "The military's translation software is appreciated. My colleagues at multiple locations have confirmed that, regardless of language, the sickness identifies itself as the same species — but not the same entity. Attempts to nail down a name have been difficult, and not just because of language barriers. There appear to be fundamental differences in cognitive models. We also think the sickness is trying to be diplomatic."

"Roger that," the Colonel replied. He was disciplined and taciturn, but there was real human concern in his eyes.

"What else have they been saying?" Cynthia asked.

"There's no sign of anything foreign in any blood samples in the world," the Doctor replied. "In fact, even patients who've passed away have had no traces of unknown microbes in their brains."

Cynthia started crying softly.

"I'm sorry," the Doctor said. "But we need to know."

"I know," was all Cynthia could manage. She sat tall, her hands in her lap, and watched her little girl.

"We are sorry for your distress," said Shannon's mouth. There was no movement in her eyelids, or even in any of the micro-muscles not absolutely necessary for speech. It was eerie, her mouth talking with no other input. It would be mechanical, except that tone and other nuances of voice came through.

"If you're hurting our Shannon…" Andrew started.

"We do not cause suffering for our hosts," her mouth

said, "but we must be brief. We dearly wish for more careful exploration and deep, diplomatic discussion. There is so much we can learn from each other. Sadly, our people are in haste."

"So are we," the Colonel said. The doctor shook her head at him.

"We will do our best to answer your most urgent questions, as we know how this must seem, but please — be concise. Our people are dying on your world, and never meant to come here."

"Then why did you?" Andrew.

"An accident. We have struggled to understand your people, and astronomical effort was required to learn enough to reach out to you through what you call your brain."

"Why haven't we found any traces of you?" asked the Doctor. "Our networks claim you're asking for help, and that you've even provided a description of yourselves."

"We fear your weapons."

"No one has authorized use of force on anyone in a coma, regardless of signs of…your people," said the Colonel. A sigh of relief from the Doctor.

"Apologies, there is much to navigate. We mean your medicines."

"You're afraid of being cured?" asked Cynthia. Her eyes were dry now. Of all the conscious people in the room, she was the most stable.

"None of us have harmed any of you. Please stop calling us a sickness. We just want to leave your world."

"Why haven't you?" Andrew tightened on Cynthia's shoulders as he spoke.

"Doctor, please summarize what our cohorts throughout the world have been telling you about us. It may clarify."

The Doctor blinked. Everyone looked at her expectantly. Taking a breath, she began: "Without any samples, we have nothing but their word to go on for a lot of it, but here goes: They're shaped roughly like 3D five-point stars, and each point is bent in a different direction. They have cell walls that include polymerized gravitons. If a germ could wear a leather jacket, these thi-...people...have gravity like studs on the jacket. Neutronium nucleus. Any microbiologist will tell you that's impossible."

"Physicists agree," the Colonel added. "The military has been coordinating with any even remotely related scientific community for the last twenty-seven hours," he replied to various glances. "On the off chance that the si-... the aliens are telling the truth."

Mouth: "Please finish, Doctor."

"They don't understand time or space the way we do. Apparently, they get around by teleporting. This term bothers them, and there are nuances mathematicians and cosmologists have debated at length. But I can't think of a better word without giving you all a crash course in a lifetime of highly advanced theories about the basics of our universe. These, uh, people, can only talk to us through patients at a minimum of twelve on the Glasgow Coma Scale score."

"I only have more questions than answers here," Andrew remarked.

"Thank you, Doctor," said what was in Shannon. "We are not here to invade. And we have much to offer. Most of your diseases we can cure, especially the ones coming from other microbes. And we have a way of digging your daughter out of the collapse of her protein-based mind."

"But…?" asked Cynthia.

"It would kill this cluster. To the last cell."

"Why would you help us? Why promise us anything, instead of taking what you want?" asked Andrew. Cynthia grabbed one of his hands and gently dug in one nail; a warning.

"Even deep in your oceans, we cannot get the kind of pressure we are used to. It's not a substitute for gravity, and we were hurt after our home neutron star exploded. It takes most of our use of dimensional knowledge and technology just to hold ourselves together. Also, we are grateful to you."

"We've heard of your talk about dimensions," the Doctor said. "Is that part of why you've been having trouble communicating with us?"

"You live in the world mostly through the study of matter – what you call chemistry – and the study of energy – what you call physics. To us, everything is one infinitely overlapping point in virtually infinite dimensions. The way that you go through so much space just to get to one point in space – instead of just being at the next point – is unintuitive. And you conceive of time as a thing that moves, has a discrete direction, and can be divided for measurement. We are fascinated and would love to learn more."

"Why are you grateful?" asked Cynthia. Andrew looked down at her in surprise.

"Art. Especially sculpture and music. We have learned much from your memories and dreams, and we find that your art has many more forms and nuances than ours. You have less humour than we do, though. And we're disappointed to see that you still use something as immature as money. Of all the peoples we've encountered, yours have been the strangest. Please help us, so we can help you. And learn. There is such beauty in learning."

"Okay, that's enough," Andrew said. "Get out of our daughter."

The Doctor looked down at her phone and her eyes widened.

"Sweetheart," Cynthia said, turning up at Andrew, "please stop. We can't ask them to kill themselves for Shannon."

"That's if we believe them," he replied.

The Colonel ducked out to receive a message. He was immediately replaced by the Sergeant.

"Why Earth?" Cynthia asked. "Why comas?"

"Less resistance," the not-Shannon replied. "We were interdimensional when our home exploded, so it wasn't there to complete the connection. From the fold of the planes we were on, yours was the closest source of observation. Which is, of course, the beacon for operating dimensions."

"Of course," Andrew snarked.

"Do you mean to say there's more intelligence out there?" asked the Doctor, her tone suddenly strained.

"In forms beyond number. Observation and intelligence are at the core of existence. Have you met nebulae yet?"

"…met them?" asked the Doctor.

The Colonel swapped back in. He made no comment, but he was tense.

"We are what you call microbial, though we still do not entirely grasp that. Your notions of size are odd. Nebulae have a different way of being. Don't talk to the Coalsack Nebula, though. That one is rude."

The parents looked at each other, then at the Doctor and the Colonel.

"…what's going on?" asked Cynthia.

"I'm sorry," said the Doctor. "We're doing what we can. People are starting to panic."

"What?" asked Andrew. "You said you controlled the allergic reaction. If these…things…can get her out of the coma. I mean, unless they caused it…"

"We needed the coma to reduce the interference enough in order to get into the brain. But please, you make our people nervous. The more you try to study us, the more it looks like you're making weapons."

"Medicine," corrected the Doctor.

"The difference is minimal to us."

"What is the panic really about?" asked Cynthia.

The Doctor hesitated.

"Some of the aliens have engaged," answered the Colonel. "Three patients were killed by their aliens so far."

"…and someone in Japan found that ultrasound kills them," the Doctor added.

"We have ultrasound equipment standing by," added the Colonel.

"Please," and there was real despair in the voice coming out of Shannon. "We have a democracy, not unlike yours."

"You're advanced aliens and you still have politics?" asked Andrew with a derisive snort.

"We haven't been able to find a better way without autocracy or some other disaster."

"…but you have militant groups," Cynthia concluded.

"Forgive them. They're scared. And – excuse our rudeness – but they don't see why we should be so worried about…primitives."

"What can we actually do for you?" asked the Doctor.

"We're not sure. But we cannot save ourselves, and we can do much for you."

Several soldiers entered the room carrying a portable ultrasound system.

"Please," said the Doctor. "There's so much we could learn!"

"We have our orders," replied the Colonel.

"If Cynthia trusts them…" Andrew said, standing between the bed and the soldiers.

"I don't know, there's a lot that's hard to prove…" Cynthia reasoned. "But there's nothing medicine can do for Shannon, is there?"

"Not even experimentation," the Doctor confirmed. "No drugs or desperate procedures. There's nothing we can do."

"Please step aside," the Colonel said. "You know we cannot risk letting them have their way. They can clearly get anywhere in the world, and we have no way of being sure why they leave no trace."

"At least hear this one out," said Cynthia.

"We can't let you take away our last chance, no matter how desperate!" Andrew said.

"We have our orders," the Colonel reminded his troops.

Cynthia, at a loss, turned to the bed. "Why aren't you saying anyth-"

"Mom?"

FIRE STEIN

"Are there any fireflies left?" asked the moss.

"Looks like they all gave up their souls to fill the Fire Stein," answered one of the trees.

"I think that's called a lantern," another tree remarked.

"It's shaped like a stein and filled with fire," retorted the first tree, "so why call it anything else?"

"I should dearly like to have some of the fireflies in this discussion," a bundle of flowers commented, "they're always so good at navigating decisions by committee."

"But we're already done!" said the second tree. "Just look at how the hair hides the face. Great job on that hair, mist."

"Thanks," said the mist, "but I'm a little worried."

"We should be fine." The moss was trying to be reassuring, though it wasn't sure if it was comforting the others or itself. "We have a real live will-o'-the-wisp in that Fire Stein!"

"Lantern."

"Whatever."

"All right," the first tree raised its voice. "Everyone sit still so we can work this out. We can't send this guardian against the humans without a face."

"We're plants," remarked the second tree. "We have to sit still."

"You know what I mean."

"We could work more on the dress…" the flowers ventured.

"I rather like it as it is," said the mist. "And-"

"You know we're all still here, right?" said the wisp.

Everyone was silent a moment.

"Now that I can sustain myself, all I need are bigger and stronger souls," said the wisp. "And I am grateful for the carrier. But we only need the humans to come close."

LIVING AND LEARNING

Jerex sat as the campfire towered in whorls of white and gold, lowering the bow in her left hand until it perched between the log and her left leg. Her right hand, an ethereal white-blue, was resting on her right knee. Aliiño and Urusawa had both cried out in surprise and mingled anger. Aliiño held a half-standing position, supported by mechanical legs with liquid metal joints. Their hands were folded atop the pack strapped to the front of their torso.

Urusawa was livid. "What was that!? We're supposed to share our stories!"

"I did," she replied. She regarded him coolly, but out of confidence in her position – not indifference to his feelings.

"We," said the warrior monk, pointing to Aliiño as he raged, "are sharing ours next! With words! How can we hear your story now that you've shot it away?"

"You won't be able to hear her over your blood pressure if you don't calm down, Oor," Aliiño intoned. Their voice had a musical resonance that thrummed like deep chords in the earth. "I'm sure she had-"

"You can't remember it now!" Urusawa's anger was a fearless panic, tinged with despair. Though dressed in the kasaya of a monk and a heavy cloak, his strength shone in the grace of his movements. This, along with their rocky surroundings, made his seething words seem louder than they were.

Orange and red roared with a voice of gold over the trio's encampment. They were on the edges of Dwarven territory, a few hours' march from the nearest entrance to the Snowflake, and surrounded on three sides by sheer rock.

"I'm keeping nothing from you!" Jerex said, her flesh hand gripping her bow more tightly. Her grey eyes hardened and her jaw tensed under the burden of her self-control.

"You'll wake the frostrees," Aliiño warned, meaning the icy forest that grew on their fourth side. Making a fire from frostree wood had taken some doing, but Urusawa had more going for him than merely his fists. Small gems glimmered on the backs of his fists and his forehead. Pouches strung about his person clinked when he moved.

Urusawa ignored their half-mechanical friend and marched up to Jerex, his yellow eyes fierce. "We all know how your arrows work," he said through gritted teeth.

Jerex stood back up to meet her friend face-to-face. Her quiver – full of regular, wooden arrows – jostled and shifted. Her bow rested almost horizontally in her left hand. Her right ethereal hand pointed a ghostly finger at the warrior, who stood at least a good half a foot lower than her. Though he was far more evenly muscled from his martial arts background, her shoulders were broader and bulkier than Urusawa's because archery was much more demanding on her tiny frame than a lot of people might imagine. Her own voice was low, cold, and menacing: "Are you so sure? It isn't like you to jump to conclusions. Are we slipping in our discipline, monk?"

Things might have gotten out of hand were it not for a sudden grip upon each of them that pulled the two apart. The neutrois member of the trio was now standing between the man and the woman. Aliiño's arms, which were of the normal flesh variety, rested a hand on the shoulder of each of their friends. The pair had been pulled apart by long thin metallic appendages that resembled spider legs.

Four such prosthetics extended from Aliiño's back, in addition to the stockier tube-shaped limbs that replaced their original legs. Their eyes were purple, which was common among hybrids like themself. They said, "Enough of this. We've come too far to bicker now. Let's return to our seats." They looked meaningfully at Urusawa while Jerex looked away with lips thinned to a line.

Urusawa took air into his nose and sighed as he returned to the rock upon which he'd perched. He sat, as one might expect, in a cross-legged position. His hands he cupped in his lap. "I want an explanation," he said as the others returned to their seats.

"Of course," Jerex replied, though frigid anger oozed from both her posture and the hardness in her eyes. "I didn't tell you beforehand, because I knew you wouldn't understand."

"That is not fair to either of us," Aliiño pointed out. They spoke each word clearly and carefully, as though they were placing pieces on a Go board.

Jerex turned her head slowly and furrowed her brow. Urusawa procured from a pack on the ground a small leather pouch. This pouch, they all knew, was filled with ashes.

The hybrid elaborated: "How long have we been travelling together now?"

"Three years," answered Jerex with a frown.

"Are we not closer friends than that?" Aliiño pressed.

Again, the archer's eyes hardened. "I knew you two – especially Oor – would not understand."

"What's that supposed to mean?" he asked in a dangerous tone.

"Why are you so touchy all of a sudden?" In this, Jerex was legitimately surprised. The monk's discipline had always served them all true, even when the other two were overcome with emotion.

"We've all picked stories that mean a lot to us, which makes us vulnerable," Aliiño surmised.

"I haven't robbed you of mine," Jerex replied.

"But you have," retorted the monk.

"He's right," Aliiño explained. "You just used a ghost arrow. We saw it. They cost you a memory."

Jerex nodded. "And you know I'd use the story I'm to offer, because I fired it with my offering."

"So if the Dragon gold is gone, and you put the memory of your story into the arrow, how is it that you haven't robbed us of your offering?" This, again, was the hybrid. They'd produced from their own pack an object containing a network of flashing tendrils: literally lightning in a bottle.

"We haven't taught each other our skillsets," Jerex pointed out. She was looking at the monk. His skill was no small thing. The Crystal Monastery taught the arduous devotion required to embody mental and physical energy into crystals and gems, like those he carried. They were manifest mastery, strength, and faith. Jerex continued with this in mind, "I don't know what Aliiño would do, Oor, but wouldn't you add one of your gems to the Ashes of the True Tree if you could?" She nodded at the pouch he held as she spoke.

Embers of anger glowed in the man as he spoke, even and measured. "I cannot put a story into them. Well, not like that, anyway."

"Can I not ask you both to trust my judgement on this?" Jerex asked, spreading her arms. Her bow she had leaned on the log beside her.

Aliiño and Urusawa looked at each other. Both looked at the archer. The hybrid sighed as the monk said, "…your faith has been true. Yet I am not satisfied."

"Fair enough," she replied. She turned to her partly mechanical friend. Their purple eyes met her grey ones. "My Dragon gold and my story have been added to the fire. Will you offer the Skyhammer?"

Aliiño stared at Jerex a moment, then they slowly stood. Each joint of every limb was liquid metal. The limbs themselves were mostly metals and metalloids, grey-silver with linings of cobalt blue or carbon black. The legs, much stockier than the four spider limbs, did not end in feet. They simply stopped. The ends of the legs could produce a variety of tools, but right now Aliiño walked upon flat ends. Their pack was strapped to their front, because most of the hybrid's back was occupied with the base of their mechanical limbs. Since the hybrid was used to quickly transporting themself on the lanky strides of the spider limbs, using their actual legs was a slower and more careful affair.

Fire gleamed in purple eyes and the metal of their body. Their spindly limbs were tucked behind them, so that their shadow looked to be wearing something triangular and ornate upon the shoulders. Thick blue-purple tree trunks stood in a pyramid of heat and gold-limned energy.

Though no one said so, everyone was surprised by how quickly the Dragon gold had melted. They'd decided upon Jerex's offering first because they expected it to take a while. Perhaps the offerings resonated. Maybe the weight of story pulsed with the world, like the energy that the monk called "chi."

He spelled it "Qi," a fact the other two did not understand.

Aliiño lifted up the bottle of Skyhammer. "You two were with me when I ventured into the Snowflake to retrieve this," they said. The Snowflake was an elaborate network of tunnels in Dwarven tundra, and it was rumoured that this network looked like a snowflake if seen from above on a map. Only Dwarves could have tunnelled in the permafrost. Or would have wanted to, for that matter. Aliiño continued, "So you know how I got this."

The other two nodded once. Storing the power of lightning gave the Dwarves powerful new methods of forging, but their system had to be cold to achieve containment. They did not share Skyhammer lightly, so the trio had had to help them rebuild a food supply system that had been damaged in the Lich War. Aliiño had leveraged connections just to get them talking to the Dwarves, who were wary of foreigners at the best of times.

Though the trio were accomplished fighters and capable travellers with unique skillsets, and the Dwarves were crippled on every level to varying degrees after the war, there was no hope of taking the Skyhammer by force. Not that they'd have wanted it that way, in any case.

The hybrid sighed. "I didn't want to tell you two about the story of how I gained the connection of the Snowflake Dwarves." Jerex and Urusawa offered their friend a solemn silence. The monk cast the archer a resentful glare. Aliiño looked down at the bottle and sniffed with amusement. "Do I open the bottle?"

They all laughed.

Urusawa rubbed his chin.

"I sent mine in with an arrow of ghost magic," Jerex conjectured, "and the fire still responded."

"At best, that was a great risk," Aliiño answered darkly.

"Maybe," said Jerex, "but I think something this important doesn't care as long as its requirements are met."

"Our gems are less about the matter they are made of and more about the potential and the dedication they contain," Urusawa added. "I was just going to throw in pouch and all, so I don't see how the magic will care about the glass of your bottle."

"Ingredients are very demanding in every science I've

encountered," Aliiño pointed out. Since half their body was made up of solid and liquid machinery, that was no small statement.

"But this isn't science," Urusawa replied.

Taking a deep breath, the hybrid threw the Skyhammer into the fire. The result was less spectacular but more unsettling than before. Other than the occasional arc of electricity that danced within the fire's bounds, and the shattering of glass, the only indication of change was a spiritual kind of static. All three of them felt it, though none of them could point to anything that they could say was happening per se. If the soul of a person could have static, then mana – the soul of the universe around them – was standing up like statically charged hair.

"I offer this story," Aliiño began.

Before the Lich War, business was booming. Aliiño's people, from the technologically advanced nation of Cheyhua, benefitted from Dwarven mining and extraction. The Dwarves, though capable of tremendous feats of manufacturing, did not fare so well with information technology. Cheyhua had long ago developed methods of harnessing blood and nerves to convey thoughts the way that a person's brain told their hands how to move.

Yet the Dwarves were stubborn when it came to sharing the mines themselves. They did not want Cheyhuan technology worked into the mechanisms of their forges and mineral extraction systems. The political landscape was full of generosity, excitement, tension, apprehension, and polite mistrust. Aliiño had had little to do with that in any direct way. They were part of a team who were building an experimental medical facility on the Tundra-

Cheyhua border.

As they worked on the facility, Aliiño developed a close friendship with a lesbian Dwarf named Brukwë. She'd thought Aliiño was also a lesbian, and things got awkward before they got better.

Dwarves and Cheyhuans made tremendous progress with the hospital, which was intended to specialize in the implementation and research of prosthetics. Brukwë was excited about this, because her father was being sustained by Elven intensive care due to his failing heart. Normally, he'd have had to say his goodbyes; the Elves did not generally share or treat with outsiders. Elven healing magic was planned to be part of the facility's operations, however, so they began offering more help as a gesture of good will.

The new technologies promised by the hospital would mean he'd be half machine. But he'd be alive. Aliiño delighted in the hope they saw in Brukwë. They didn't realize her feelings continued unabated, well after the two had discussed the nature of their friendship. She kissed them once, after a particularly trying achievement when a team of twenty were assembling a life support network.

Right now, Aliiño was standing before the fire, gold-hued and electric, and tears streamed freely down their face. "I got angry at her at the time. It was stupid of me," the hybrid said. Neither archer nor monk spoke; they weren't sure if it would be right. "We got into a fight. She stormed off. I continued working. I didn't have any of this at the time," and the hybrid gestured at their mechanical accoutrements. They stopped a moment when they looked down at their metallic legs.

Silence.

Then Aliiño continued with their story.

The medical facility, it turned out, was hotly contested by several groups. Rumours ran like wildfire, most of them ludicrous; illegal experimentation on people, a drug underground, something about the procedures causing leprosy. Even celebrities got in on it, claiming to be "gurus" (whatever that meant) and opposing the implementation of biomechanical medicine.

Brukwë had stormed off right into the clutches of a faction of extremists who were in the middle of trying to sabotage the hospital. She managed to sound the alert in time for everyone to panic. Dwarves and Cheyhuan humans alike were abandoning their posts, getting into confused fights, joining the invaders without realizing what they'd agreed to, and generally causing a wholesale disaster.

"I couldn't save Brukwë," Aliiño choked out. "I could only r-read her… her lips before the explosion took her. 'I love you,' she said. I…" the hybrid swallowed. They spoke in a quaking, not-quite-crying loud whisper for the rest of their story. "I got the king of the Dwarves out. He'd been there on a diplomatic mission. I was part of the battle that pushed out the extremists and got everyone into some kind of order. I helped pull the Cheyhuan president out of the forges. She lost an arm and part of her face, but she lived. Some of the machinery gave way, and my spine was broken."

Aliiño looked up to the sky. They looked at Urusawa, and they looked at Jerex. They stared into the fire. "When I came to, the facility had been completed. The president and the king had personally funded… this," and again they indicated their limbs. "As reward for my courage and accomplishments."

The hybrid lowered their head. "More than just recovering my legs, they gave me a variety of tools and these," they said, lifting their spider limbs, "a process that must have cost millions. But Brukwë was gone. Her father asked to be taken off life support when he found out. To compensate for the lost costs, the hospital was privatized. The Elves wanted nothing to do with that. Now only the wealthy get prosthetics at all, and none of them are equipped like me."

The monk held his stoic composure, but there was sadness in his eyes. Jerex looked down at her hands, flesh entwined with ghost. The neutrois finished their story: "I left after launching a political rebellion to right the economic inequality. The president was impeached for supporting me. The system made me sick. The Lich War gave the king an excuse to ignore my pleas.

"…so here I am," finished Aliiño. Without ceremony now, they used their long spindly limbs to return themself to the patch of ground where they half-knelt, half-sat on tireless metal legs.

Since the monk and the archer had been curious about the hybrid's parts for a long time, the trio talked it through until a few jokes came out. Acceptance and support were the words of the hour. Urusawa eventually stepped forward and threw his pouch of ashes into the fire without ceremony. As with Aliiño, he didn't explain how he'd gotten the Ashes of the True Tree. The three of them had been together for that as well.

The Elves did not have the means to fight the plague that was spreading through the Human lands in the south, but they did what they could to help. When the trio showed up, and explained what they were trying to do, the Elves were sceptical. A True Tree was hard to grow, and it had to be tended a long time for its magic to be strong enough to help them. They knew what it meant to burn a True Tree.

Few believed the stories about the Phoenix.

At first, they were turned away. Jerex was determined. By that point, they'd already helped her acquire the Dragon gold. She would not walk away from this in shame. Urusawa leveraged the history of the Crystal Monastery only on the trio's second attempt, as he felt it was an abuse of good will. It was the monks who'd stopped the Humans from committing genocide against the Elves fifteen hundred years ago. Most of the Elves who had survived the encampments and cultural occupation still lived.

In recognition of the Monastery's philanthropy, the Elves acquiesced on the condition that the ashes would be accepted through the Elven Forest and the Crystal Monks. Which meant more wasted time. Three weeks of paperwork later, the trio finally had the second offering. The plague was, by that point, officially considered a state of emergency, and not less than four Human countries and one Elvish nation were quarantined.

The famous alchemist, Ulsar Denturoth, had lived and died in one of those Human countries. He'd reputedly been on the verge of discovering a cure when his laboratory had been set alight by a mob. They thought he was withholding painkillers. This also did not make it to Urusawa's tale, because Denturoth's death was why the trio were working together.

Instead, the monk said, "I had to do some good. With the plague running amok and the alchemist dead, I had to contribute, because…"

He told the story of his sister.

Her name was Shanichi, and he was fiercely proud of her. He told of her exploits for animal rights, and her vegetarian lifestyle. They sometimes argued because he disagreed about not eating meat, but she did give him a passion for cooking. He used meat in his cooking, but only if he'd been the one to raise the animal. Shanichi rubbed off on him a little. She supported his choice to go to the Monastery, even when the family wanted him to stick to the tannery, because she understood his conviction.

He'd been ordained as a monk for about five years when he learned the plague had started in remote river villages. These were far from his home. He cared, of course. He spearheaded his Monastery's efforts to produce crystals and gems that would help fight the plague. Seven months later, his sister had it. A month before that, the alchemist had died.

It took Urusawa two hours to tell his story – or rather, his sister's – in full. To his knowledge, she was still alive. When the ashes hit the flame, it at first shrank slightly and the wood that fed it seemed to become more vibrantly bluish-purple. It was as though the frostree wood gained new life even as it burned. As Urusawa's lips closed on the final word of his story, a great heat wave hit them all, and it was air more than fire that launched the trio backward.

When they recovered, they found before them an unmistakable being.

It was less a bird made of fire than a firestorm shaped like a bird. Its pinions glimmered with the delicious sheen of gold, and its yellow eyes were electric with fire and light. Now the circle of rocks contained only charred wood that had surrendered its colour to black.

The Phoenix flapped about the campsite three times, then settled on the ground outside the circle and folded its blazing wings. It glared at Jerex.

"I do not appreciate what you've done."

Aliiño and Urusawa stared at the great sparking creature in awe, and when its words registered, they looked at the archer for explanation.

"You have within you my story," the archer said.

"All three, yes," it said. It spread its wings to indicate the hybrid and the monk. "But I cannot leave until I share the story you put in me."

"I figure it's only fair," Jerex answered. "We're all of us vulnerable. Sharing a story powerful enough for the Divine Wind is dangerous, and leaves us all naked. And we don't even know who – or what – you really are. What's keeping you from leaving us, from rejecting our request? By all that lives, you could even go on a rampage. None of us have met a Phoenix before, and legends change with time."

The entity frowned. At least, that was the energy they got from it. Certainly there was no change in its beak. All three of them felt the static of its wrath, like a whole forest that remembered every ember and every axe. "Binding me with your story forces me to stay until I've shared it.

Why would I help you after that?"

"Why would we give you life at all, if not for what you can grant us?" It was Urusawa, of all people, who stood up for Jerex's decision. "We've called the Divine Wind to feed your everlasting fire. Do you not feel the faith of the world, all the magics of life?"

"I feel the prevailing winds," it answered. "I feel them like everything you've ever loved. Yet I only feel them now. Your voices are as music to me, though I have all your memories of all the people who have ever spoken to you. I remember them, but I have not heard them myself." It shifted about. "Why am I without a name?"

The trio looked between each other in confusion.

"I am born!" declared the Phoenix. "I have a Dragon's pride, and its sense of self. Greed is an extension of self, but so is love, and power! This I get from Dragon gold. The ashes of a bastion of life are also within me, and about me, and before me for every memory yet to be! And do I not spark with heavens and every beginning that ends!"

"I offer you my story, and Dragon gold," answered Jerex.

"I offer you my story, and Skyhammer," answered Aliiño.

"I offer you my story, and True Tree Ashes," answered Urusawa.

The Phoenix regarded each in turn. "Your story has blocked my name," it said to the archer. "Why would I bring back your alchemist, when I am nameless?"

"I am sorry, great Phoenix," Jerex replied. She wasn't used to being this formal, but somehow she didn't feel she could use slang with such a creature. "I meant only to have you share my story long enough to listen to our hope."

Three circles of fire shot up. One, innermost, was gold. Second was grey and dim, and seemed to absorb more light than it gave out. The third was blue, and flowed in lines shot with white. Neither archer, monk, nor hybrid had any means of escape. Yet they did not feel a threat.

"I would not have listened," admitted the Phoenix.

"You don't care?" asked Aliiño despondently.

"You are people," the bird said. One eye alone looked at them. There was no way for anyone to see it, but somehow they all knew: it was looking at the neutrois. "People live short lives. Most of them meaningless. I never die. Why do you matter to me?"

"What did you mean about your name?" asked Urusawa.

This was not a response the Phoenix would have expected. "Are my kind not born with names?"

The trio looked amongst each other and shrugged. The circles of fire cast them all in an otherworldly hue, but the heat was not unbearable. After the cold of the nearby Tundra, it was somewhat refreshing.

"…I see," it said.

"My name is my own," said Aliiño.

Man, woman, and firebird turned their attention to the hybrid.

"I was not born to this name," they explained. "The 'nyo' sound is a masculine name convention in Cheyhua, and the 'a-lee' sound is feminine. Aliit is a female name and Deño a male. I took this name for myself when I came to terms with who I am."

"You're saying I should make my own name," surmised the Phoenix.

"What story did I give you?" asked Jerex.

Urusawa's expression was hard to describe.

"In your country," it said, wondering what this had to do with its name, "there is a practice. You may take up the mantle of sacrifice, and offer something irreplaceable in exchange for living access to your soul. Some people give up pets to get a familiar. You chose your hand. Through this power, you had the ability to give up a memory to create a magic arrow. These ghost arrows could do incredible things, depending upon the power of the memory you gave for them."

Aliiño's frown had been deepening until they had to speak. "This is not a story."

"Everything starts somewhere," replied the Phoenix. Then it continued: "You used this power to fight the Dragon, alongside your friends here, to get a coin of its gold." It looked at Aliiño. "She forgot her childhood friend to protect you from Dragonfire." It looked at Urusawa. "She forgot her favourite song to give you the dream that inspired your speech to the Elves."

The monk was astounded. "YOU SHOT ME IN MY SLEEP!?"

Jerex scratched behind her ear self-consciously. "I was trying to help?" she offered with uncharacteristic meekness.

Taking each in turn, the Phoenix looked at all of them. Then it said, "Jerex made the sacrifice to gain that power so she could restore her grandmother's memories."

And then it explained.

It spoke quickly, because it had so much to say.

It described, for almost an hour, what this had meant to Jerex. How she'd lived with her grandmother for most of her life, and how she'd had to watch it happen. One day at a time. Sometimes it was just mixing up the utensils. Sometimes she mixed up names, or forgot who Jerex was. Sometimes she was found wandering the forest, as no one had seen her leave the village.

It was like watching the woman become a ghost. Watching her fade. Giving her gifts she wouldn't remember. Seeing her get lost trying to read a sundial. Helping her navigate the labyrinth that each meal had become. One of the hardest things was having her grandmother fill the gaps with fiction.

"A wandering minstrel came by for lunch today," her grandmother had said to make conversation. It was winter. The minstrels only came by their cluster of villages in the summer, because the roads were impassable in winter.

Jerex said as much.

"He'd gotten stuck in Stold," her grandmother had replied. Stold was the neighbouring village. "He came by to give a gravesong while you were hunting."

No babies had died since Jerex left for the hunt. She always checked for such news on her return. But a gravesong was the way of the villages for the passing of a child, and every winter at least two or three times one village would dig its way to another looking for someone who at least had a voice for the child's soul – if not the right words.

Her grandmother's stories were plausible, albeit false, and filled the gap in the elder's mind where the day's events should have been.

After so many stories like that, Jerex made the sacrifice. Every day until the end, Jerex gave a memory so her grandmother would remember.

"You named your hands," the Phoenix said at last.

Eyes closed, lips trembling, Jerex held up her left hand. The one that still had flesh. "Living," the Phoenix said. And as she lifted the right, it added, "Learning."

The circles of fire vanished.

"Hope," it said, looking at Urusawa. "In the language of the Divine Wind, it is called Yim."

"Compassion," it said, looking at Aliiño. "To the Divine Wind, Elch."

"Love," it said, looking at Jerex, "is known to the Divine Wind as Aana."

"My name," declared the Phoenix, "is Yimelchaana."

Their eyes were filled with lightning.

Ashes consumed all sound.

And their skin became gold, majestic and unfeeling.

The moon was high in a starless night. They all shivered with the sudden shock of firelessness. They could see each other in the moonlight. The glimmer of gems, metallic limbs, and a ghostly hand. The circle of rocks was empty.

Their breath came in scintillating clouds.

It took them three months to return to the southern countries. They first heard rumours two weeks prior, but it was the full three months before they were sure.

The Alchemist was reborn. People said it was a meteor. A screaming fire spewed from the sky. Ulsar Denturoth emerged from a city of ruins and ghosts. He carried vials of life, and he told everyone who drank of them:

"I had a strange dream about a bird made of fire. It told me to spread the flames of life that I make in these vials. So run! All of you, touch everyone you can. Run! Hope is a thing that spreads!"

When she heard these words, spread by the heralds and the joyous survivors, Jerex looked down at her hands. She put them together, as if noticing them for the first time.

And she could only feel one of them.

Author's Note: *This story was originally published in* Fantasy from the Rock, *by Engen Books. While I often work to the last minute, it's because I'm always re-thinking and tinkering. This story was a rare case in which I didn't even start until five hours before submissions closed. I sent it in with ten minutes to spare. Bam!*

ROCKET SCIONS

"We should let the free market sort it out."

"You want us to buy wombs?"

"Why not?"

"Should we have all the female researchers here do our housework while we're at it?"

"What the devil are you talking about? Stay focused, boy."

"I'm a woman!"

"Details."

"…"

"Now, it will put a dent into our budget. Unless we can get them by donation. Can we get them by donation, do you think?"

"Getting a hysterectomy isn't like going to the blood clinic, doctor."

"True. Some people are afraid of needles. You can use gas for the hysterectomy, though."

"…you, I…but…never mind."

"Focus."

(I'll give you focus)

"Sorry?"

"Nothing."

"Anyway, have the team get together. Iron out the details. What are you sighing about?"

"Nothing. Don't worry about it."

"Right. This should be really easy for the marketing department."

"Easy? Do I even want to ask?"

"Of course you do. And here's the answer: getting to have your name on the first vessel to Alpha Centauri. Can you imagine?"

"No."

"Good answer! Neither can I. Oh, how I wish I could be there! To set foot…"

"We can agree on that, at least. Pity about the fifty light-years. Still, it is exciting: a living rocket, a travelling ecosystem. Public transit, eat your heart out!"

"Sadly, yes. No diet will get another fifty years out of me."

"Did…you…tune me out?"

"Just getting the rocket ready will take years. Do you have the stem cell samples yet?"

(First name rights. That'll show you.)

"Hm?"

"Nothing. I'll get started on the grant applications."

LIFE ACCORDING TO THE PUBLIC

His coat was too thin.

Doug got by on sneakers and relied upon the immortality of his jeans. The overpass of Pitts Memorial highway loomed ahead of him as he made his way across the last of the intersections that would lead back up to it. Anyone who wanted to drive up there from here would have to either turn around or continue to the turnoff beyond the Waterford.

He was tense with the cold, as he hadn't been walking long enough to adapt to it. Whenever anyone asked, he just said that he liked to go out under-equipped because, "Your heat catches up with you when you're movin'." He had enough quarters and a loonie for one of the overpriced bags of chips at the side of the bar.

They called him Howser, and he couldn't take beer money out of the rent. So he told everyone he was going dry for the lifestyle choice. Doug was walking to the Station, a pub under the overpass, and he had a young face for his age. Since the cupboards were thin and bare at home, so was his face. This added to the air of youth, and his eyes and hair played along for a vague, bargain-bin Doogie Howser look.

It hadn't taken long for moisture to sneak out of the snow and through the working class of his shoes, despite his careful efforts to dodge the sloppiest areas. Snowmageddon was over, and there were more hard-lined streetside cliffs of dry-ish snow than he'd expected for March in St. John's, but it was still March in St. John's.

Being out with his friends took the sting off of working retail. He'd had such plans. No letters after his name, but he figured the results of his work would be enough. His software stuff was solid, but hardware was his strong suit. This crisp winter night, salt glistening in the nose because the harbour wasn't far behind him, felt like a distant ache. Where was the hum of motherboards and electrical cooling fans, with its embrace like Nan's gingerbread?

Only the sliding hush of passing cars put a sense of landscape in the air. He was tired. Even when he'd been in the house, all dry socks and pockets still tinkling with change, his feet jangled with the dings and bumps of cash registers. They spent the day eeling their way down to the tips of his toes. He fantasized about spending a triple-digit amount of money on shoes. Half his month's grocery bill, for shoes. Lunacy. But the feeling, he'd daydreamed of it: like stepping on clouds. None of—

"HOWSER!" hit him just before the heat of the air as he stepped past the door. Around one corner to his right rang the rolling digital carousel of VLTs. Once past the entry hallway, the machines were louder — and the bar straight ahead. Standing beside it like its irreverent knight was a tall man, the one who'd called his name.

There were others, of course — and they ranged from bald to $300 at the salon. The ones who weren't part of the VLTs or just barflies with nowhere better to be were going to be on the enemy teams. "Hey," Doug started, catching himself before he used a word like "man" or "dude." Duncan didn't like those kinds of words. Doug never really got his head around why. Now that he thought on it, Duncan was the only one in the group who didn't have a nickname.

"WHATTAYA AT, LUH?" Duncan was like a hardened cell phone stuck on CapsLock. He probably had one, all dun colours and hard edges. But somehow it made sense to expect pink stickers. Instead of the plaid a person of his build and temperament should have been wearing, he was in loafers without socks, slacks with the hems rolled up, and a black shirt with the top two buttons undone.

"Still tryin' to find you a hat," Doug teased as he got his traditional bag of Cheetos and staked out a table with Duncan. They grabbed another chair to make four. Duncan sat with a bottle of Black Horse, facing the entrance. On the far wall to Duncan's left was the projector screen the trivia host would be using. Ahead, just past the entrance to the room and on the left, was the bar.

"Cowboy? Trilby? Fedora?" Duncan asked with a grin. The lines of his face were leathery and pronounced, sitting upon the foundation of his beard like weather-beaten support beams with no actual building above them. Doug chomped on a Cheeto and seemed to be thinking about his answer. Duncan slammed both palms on the table. "BERET!" he declared. "It'll be GREAT!"

"You'll either need an art or a school," Doug said.

"Maybe even military. Berets come with responsibilities."

Duncan barked a laugh. It was rounded at the cheeks, the lips forming an "O" even as the "HA!" came out. Inwardly, Duncan knew his laughs only had so much ammunition. He never let on. "Catch is goin' good these days, if you're not afraid to mix n' match. Decent lobster haul comin' up, I reckon. How was Bitters?"

Doug shrugged. "Great food. Lots of structure, probably all the grad students trying to make life feel like their programs. All the computer questions were about either software or…"

Doug went on for a while about the company he kept and the frustrations he thought he was hiding. He asked about how long Duncan had been kicking around before he'd showed up. What Doug didn't ask was how his fisher friend always seemed to have beer money. Dingy house run roughshod, "neether" car to his name, limited wardrobe. But beer dollars aplenty.

Duncan gave noncommittal answers and watched as people filled in. He'd been in court a few times — jury duty, called in as a witness for some disputes regarding fish stocks or a boating incident, only once for a crime on his own hands — and had come to find that he was seeing it everywhere now. As long as people were entering for the proceedings, it all seemed so…anonymous. But somehow, once the process started, you got faces and names locked into place.

When the other two members of their circle showed up, it was Duncan who waved them over. Howser was being Howser. Duncan had seen that look in some of his buddies out at sea: this man was here in order to not be somewhere else. That meant that it was the somewhere else — and not the man — who was really sitting with him now. It made him want to dress differently or give Howser some pointers on the subject.

Instead, they all took up the answer sheet and dove into Round 1. The category was cars. All of the players sat, divided into teams that were strewn about like balls on a billiard table. Howser was clockwise from Duncan. Counter-clockwise, going from Duncan's right and following the curve of the table, were Serenity (or "Wren") and Gwendolyn. As the host put up a picture of a carburetor and told the participants to write what the part was called, Duncan grabbed the sheet and slapped in the answer.

"We will need an extra pencil," Wren put in. Her voice was quiet, but it carried to the others at the table. While piano was her forte, she sang enough to know about voice projection. Duncan cast a sidelong glance at her, noting the stiffness of her posture.

"If I can keep me pencils goin' on maps and papers, wit' the boat shiftin' and storms hollerin', I can manage well enough here," Duncan said. He was less boisterous now, but he still spoke with the weight of old bones and heavy nets. Serenity, he noticed, wore wire-rimmed glasses, a ponytail, and a turtleneck sweater. Her gloves were thin leather, not too warm to wear indoors. In fact, her face was the only bare skin — and even then, she wore makeup.

"Easy, friends," Howser said affably. "No need for a bar brawl." But he was only looking at Duncan.

"There are two basic kinds of engine," the host was saying.

Duncan had turned his attention in the direction of the projector screen, openly unconcerned. Gwendolyn, known to her friends as Doll or Dolly, held up a pen and stuck out her tongue when Duncan narrowed his eyes at her. "How's that collection going?" she asked.

"...nt you to tell me what a bottom-heavy engine gives you. It's a one-word answer."

Duncan's work had given him some appreciation for engines, though he wasn't exactly a car person. He was the one providing most of the answers in this category, except for some of the questions about the fancy electronics. Howser had that one. The fisher regarded the event planner. "What's that, Dolly?"

"The star-chart stuff you do," she said with a smile.

"Yeah!" Doug said. "I saw that in the paper. You've got a backyard museum!"

"Well, I don't know about that," Duncan answered. His pride was obvious. "But sure, I got an astrolabe the other day. Still diggin' about freezin' the balls off a brass monkey."

Wren's head tilted back just a smidge. None of the others noticed the tightening between her eyes and her lips, but Duncan had seen it often enough. This wasn't some kind of ergonomics routine; she was hurting somewhere, and staying stiff to hide it. The host moved into the next category: Weird Signs.

"What do you mean, digging about it?" Doll put in. She was an amateur geometer; she needed to know where everything fit.

"Okay: back in the cannon days, there was this big brass circle rack you put the cannonballs on called the brass monkey," Duncan set in. Doug rolled his eyes. Wren was watching the images and filling the answer sheet when she could. Only her neck tilted. Dolly had forgotten about the game. "When it got real cold," Duncan continued, "the brass would pull tighter than the iron of the balls. So it would squeeze them out, like when you're holding a wet bar of soap. They'd go everywhere!"

Doug ventured guesses with Wren about one of the answers. Gwendolyn frowned. "I suppose brass shrinkage would be greater than iron. I've never heard this story before. Why don't we see it in, you know, boat exhibits and documentaries and stuff?"

"Most sailors know that story. It's where the whole phrase comes from. Not as vulgar as all that!" Duncan declared. "They're surprisingly hard to find, though."

The host said, "This category I call 'Paving the Way,'" and went on to ask a question about cobblestones.

"Why are they so hard to find?" Dolly asked. "Seems to me there'd be plenty of them in sunken ships, museums, old warehouses."

"You'd think," Duncan said. "Just can't seem to get my hands on any, though. Bookworms can't even find records of 'em!"

"Most historians believe that the second great plague in human history, called the Black Death, was spread along what road?" the host asked.

"That reminds me," Howser put in. "I finished a woman's computer build for her the other day. She worked in news or something…"

Wren despaired, and that slid her attention into mental culverts and ditches. Despite the cars and sidewalks, despite the way that roads stitched together communities, it felt to her like they really just hemmed people in. Which side of the tracks was she really on, or was she just tied to them?

"What's that gotta do with a disease superhighway?" Duncan asked with a grin. He noticed that Wren was staring into space and looked at her until she realized she was being watched and had to come back to reality.

Doug, meanwhile, continued: "There's talk of a new disease. They're calling it coronavirus. I looked it up on Reddit after, and oh, man."

Duncan frowned at being called "man."

Doll added, "Yeah, it's been causing all kinds of stir in some of the trade circles coming out of China. Italy's having lots of trouble, so the word goes. I was working on a presentation with the Board of Trade a couple of days ago, they were talking."

"Lots of talk about quarantines. Economies are looking sketchy in a few places," Doug remarked.

The conversation jumped between the novel coronavirus, trivia about pavement and road construction, and a plethora of rabbit holes and asides until they got to the intercession. Wren went directly to the bathroom. She couldn't stay long. Appearances. She'd only had one glass of wine. It wasn't great, but there was only so much a downtown bar could do for a wino. She relieved herself and checked her make-up in the mirror. No evidence of the bruise. She'd thought that was why Duncan kept looking at her, but no.

She left the bathroom, absorbed in thought. She was free now. Her husband paid her way when her music earnings fell short. He got her connections. Opportunities. Flights, anywhere she needed to be. He hadn't meant it, and she'd been clumsy to fall. The worst of it was in the back muscles, just over the kidneys, because of how she landed. He was perfect for her. Everyone has their blips.

"Miss?" She blinked. "Oh, yes, thank you," she said as she accepted the glass of water from the bartender. She left a tip when he turned away, feeling guilty for not buying another drink. And grateful that she could still look young enough to be called "miss." She'd assumed her husband came from a home with an alcoholic. Hadn't thought to ask, but his need to measure drinks — and know where and when — seemed reasonable in that light.

She tried not to think about the satisfaction that her gloves hid her wedding ring, and returned to the table as the host was chatting with Doug and Dolly. Duncan just seemed to be taking it all in. He looked away when she met his eyes. She realized she was the only one at the table whose name — or nickname — started with a different letter.

"I went looking for it a while back," Dolly said as Wren took her seat. "It's more complicated than you might think. Yeah, it means 'three ways' or 'three roads,' but it was also part of Roman education. Kinda like undergrad, as far as I can make it."

"That makes it less random…" the host mused. Now that he was up close, he wasn't some ephemeral entity no one looked at in the dark room while they focused on answers and arguments. He was bald with the dark tan of an outdoor labourer, wearing cologne and a leather jacket that matched the scent.

"So you're saying that it could mean 'something un-dergrads might know?'" Doug asked.

"What are you talking about?" Wren asked.

"Where the word 'trivia' comes from," Duncan put in.

"Looks about that time, boss!" someone shouted from two tables over.

"Oh!" the host said, checking his watch. "All right, folks, our next category is Street Life."

The generalized background of a bar crowd became the specific noise of drinking competitors in a matter of moments as the next set of questions went along.

"So I see your make-up game is on point," Dolly said, looking over at Wren as the host repeated all the questions in the category before moving on to the next.

Serenity lifted a hand to her throat well. "Thank you! Yeah, I learned it for performances. Mostly just used it for that for years. But lately I've been kinda playing with it some more. Even checked out tricks on Youtube."

If Doll caught the lie in that, she didn't show it. "I'd like to see some of those videos, maybe compare notes. Been thinking about working it into some of my event planning, having the vendors all on the same page and what-not."

"I'd have to go digging for the specifics," Wren said, hoping she was concealing her discomfort with that idea, "but I'd be happy to. The lips, in particular, look like your element." She unconsciously clasped her hands together on the table, as though she were a dedicated student.

"Lovely!" Gwendolyn said. She'd have to leave her questions at that, for now. She wanted very much to know about Serenity's change in dress. The woman wore darker, more form-fitting outfits lately. Next to no skin exposure, and gone were the days of practical heels. Now she seemed to have a smaller variety of flats, sneakers, ankle-high boots, and leather shoes. Still tasteful, but manageable for more physical exertion. Not that that was the reason. Wren wasn't a jogger.

Why would a pianist need to run?

"Next up," the host declared, "is a category you're probably expecting from me."

"What do songs have to do with the road?" someone said.

"I was gonna have a bonus question about tonight's theme," the host said, eyeing whoever it had been.

"Just can't wait to get on the road again..." Duncan sang. His voice was a bit booming for the vibe of the song, but not too bad for all that. "The wife I love is making music..." A few people burst out laughing.

"...what?" he demanded of his audience.

"It's life, not wife," the host said. "But I like the way you think!" That got a few chuckles, too.

Wren raised a brow.

Now Doug watched Duncan as the category went on. A snippet of "Copperhead Road" came from the speakers. Wren and Duncan bobbed or swayed with it. The fisher always seemed to be grinding an edge of some kind. Whether he was out fishing, working the boats farther out to sea, collecting his old-school GPS (as Doug thought of the astronavigation), or going to his cabin in the woods. Even smoking a cigar surrounded by earth and sky. It was hard to tell if the most important thing in the world to Duncan was to keep moving or to find peace and quiet.

Or maybe the two were the same to him.

The answer sheet danced between all four teammates for this round. Different songs connected with different ones. Doug was the only one who recognized Metallica's "Wherever I May Roam," but it was also the only answer he knew. He'd heard some of the other tunes, but didn't have titles or band names.

He found himself wishing he was in his basement, working on his indie video game development or experimenting with contraptions distantly related to the Raspberry Pi. "I miss the scene at the Rose & Thistle," he said. He leaned forward to do so; he didn't want his voice going past the table.

"I mean, it's not so bad here..." Doll put in. Maybe that's what had been tugging at her. Wren's style changes, Doug's weird mishmash of outgoing and aloof, something subtle about Duncan. Maybe she was getting to know them better, seeing them in ways a passerby missed. Maybe it was just this place, and the others weren't into it.

"I'm with you, though," Duncan added. "Nudding 'gainst the establishment. It's the people, I figger."

Wren nodded once, slowly.

"Urban Legends will wrap things up tonight," the host said as he started in on the next projected slides.

This one gave the group more trouble. Dolly grouched at one point about "superstition." Duncan, meanwhile, was getting fidgety. Doug was keeping him in his peripheral vision. Dolly, at least, was all in. And Duncan himself was still eyeing Serenity. Her outfits had a bit more of a masculine flair compared to her previous tendency toward skirts, dresses, scarves, and shawls. He wondered if she lived as he did.

When Duncan was at his cabin, he felt he could safely wear the women's clothing he owned. But he wasn't a cross-dresser. Transvestites dressed as something they weren't. At least, that was how he thought that worked. But he only put on a dress when he was actually a woman. He didn't know how to explain that to anyone, didn't have the vocabulary for "gender-fluid." But going to the cabin frustrated him. It was just a different kind of hiding.

So he was a loud, cussin' drinker.

"This," said the host as he flicked up a slide image of the underside of a motorcycle, "is a special kind of bell. It has to be given by a loved one; you can't put it on your motorcycle yourself. What's it called?"

No one in the group knew the answer.

As they continued through the questions, Dolly tapped her immaculate nails on the table and remarked, "I hate knowledge gaps."

Doug blinked. "Aren't you all hands-on?"

Gwendolyn stared. "...you make that sound like it's some kind of contradiction."

"This is trivia. Yeah, I know what we said earlier about what the word might mean," he said, vaguely sensing that a predatory pounce was incoming, "but it's just...you like stuff you can use."

"Everything can be useful," she said breezily. Whatever danger had been there dispersed like a cloud of vapour. "You just don't know it yet."

"Huh?" Doug said.

"The unknown can be scary," Wren — of all people — joined in. "But it's also got some adventure in it. Y'know, the travel bug and all that." Her fingernails, well-kept but artless, rained some melody known only to her just above the tabletop.

"This calls for SHOTS!" Duncan added, slamming his hand on the table along with his boisterous emphasis. The next team over jumped in their seats and scowled at him.

"I lost count!" one of them lamented.

Doug was counting up their score.

"You want anything, Howser? I'm buyin'!"

He thought real hard about that. But he couldn't jump to free stuff too quickly. The math would be a little obvious. "No, thanks."

"Don't see why they have to wait so long to tally it all up," Dolly muttered. The host was off by the VLTs, just out of view from most of this room, chatting with someone who was also out of sight. A swarm kept Duncan from making swift work of the bar.

"So it's not about winning with you?" Doug said to Dolly as he wrote their team total.

"More about the learning," she said. "And having an excuse to spend time with you losers. What're we calling our team, anyway?"

"We should really just stick to a name," Wren said. "I don't like trying to win with that. I'd rather...you know…"

"Arrive like a band?" Doug suggested.

Duncan set down four full shot glasses. "Yellowbelly tomorrow?"

Two of the others muttered about checking their schedules. Doug would have the next day off. If he spent the whole of it on his games and tech, he'd have to start listening to his own thoughts sooner or later.

"Unless work calls me in, I'm down," he said. But he nudged away the shot glass.

IN DEFERENCE

She took in a stray dog.

Now she was wandering the woods, sticking to the paths. Dresses like hers were ill-suited to shrubbery and her shoes were no better for all the mossy, uneven terrain. But (even at crossings) no signs were in evidence. Didn't all roads have signs? Certainly, forest paths were primitive, but people used the wooded ways. Why would there be no signs?

She had no bell, no trumpet, no handmaiden to run or call out for her. And who would listen? There were stories about princesses with animals to do their clothes and hair, but that was apparently far away. Or long ago. Or both.

She was having trouble retracing things. When were days not months, once you had enough of them? It had to have started with the dog. Adorable, didn't look terribly hungry. Hurt, though.

Scared.

She couldn't resist. So she had the castle seer thrown out (what good was a prophet or a sibyl who couldn't foresee something as life-changing as that lap-loving little beauty?) and had the abode entirely redone for the dog.

Then came the messenger.

Right now, she could not see or smell the smoke. There were no more cries, she tasted nothing but nuts and berries, and felt little other than the weight of the road on her feet.

Back then, the messenger talked about the dog. Neighbouring kingdom. Demands. She'd been herself and righteous and had the man's marriage between head and shoulders annulled.

Where was the stray?

JACK HAS BEEN STOCK

His last sight was the floating door, his lover looking over its edge. Her face was blurred by the surface of the water. Only the moonlight, and the failing lights of the sinking ship in the distance, gave her any form. Around him, there was only blackness.

Around him, there was only blackness.

Before, he couldn't breathe because of water. But this was earth. Panicked, he scrambled. It wasn't long before he burst forth from the soil, coughing and fraught — but relieved. Out of the corner of his eye, he noticed activity around him. There were vague figures, spaced out and labouring. It seemed that everything — not just the sky — was overcast. Dreariness blurred everything together, like a bruise made of the shades of fog.

Was he bruised? No. Just body weight on his hands and feet, the echo of cortisol pulsing in the soil under his fingernails. Beneath him, his hands were greyscale. So were his arms, even with the duck cloth work shirt. He could've sworn it had colour.

Focus. What was before him got more attention than

his surroundings. The extra details were still smeared, perhaps even crumpled. He became aware that there was something nearby and had to palm around to level himself with it.

> "Here Lies Jack
> At the end of his song,
> Without even a cow to sell"

Jack stared. "What in blue blazes is this? What cow?"

As his brain harped upon the words, he became aware of a faint glow around him. Was it coming from the tombstone? From his…? He shuddered and did not look down. Standing up, he turned on the spot to examine the glow.

It couldn't be.

It was a beanstalk. A spectral imitation of one, at least. Blue-tinged white, it didn't look to be entirely present. Maybe it was made of something he'd never seen before, or maybe it was sheer presence. At first Jack thought he was looking at shaped, glowing fog. But it was more like glass if it could somehow be gas instead of solid. He'd never have thought that something could be both eerie and charming.

He was already miles upward, cloud flooding his vision and land sinking away, before he realized that he was moving up the beanstalk as though it were a tube. Before him was a hole in the clouds. It didn't open any wider or move in any way. All evidence suggested he'd crest the edge of the gap to find himself above the clouds. That would be about as logical as everything else so far.

It was not to be. He soon stood upon poorly swept

hardwood floorboards. While there was colour here, everything still had a crumpled quality. A meshed wastepaper basket loomed over him on his right. Beyond that, across floorboards stretching like plains, was a geography of bookshelf that extended past all reason.

While his new surroundings encroached upon him with vaulting darkness, he became increasingly aware that this wasn't a wooden cavern — smell and atmosphere notwithstanding. To his left, what he had taken for a pillar was in fact the leg of a chair.

Near it and before him was a different leg. Foot, slippers, pyjamas, and all.

The owner of the leg rumbled from far above.

From the distance, beyond what he now realized was a gargantuan writing desk, came sounds that were not quite music. Like the sky streaming over a bed of crystalline beads, it was the sound of harp strings — but at the cadence of speech. Jack never got to properly work out what he was hearing before he found himself flying back to the hole and through the beanstalk.

Instead of falling, though, he now found himself in a world clear enough to be reality.

"Yee-haw!" someone shouted nearby.

Jack looked around. No longer distracted by the *everywhere* of what was happening, he saw that he was part of a group of bandits on horseback. They were approaching a train. No more crumpling, but there was a dusty yellow-brown plain and a chugging train. Gunfire. A woman was frantically gesturing in a window. Classic frontier-style twill jacket and skirt were normal enough in grey, but the rest of her was grey too. As though she belonged in a black-and-white movie. Was she trying to warn him? Someone slid open a train car door and tossed out an off-white canvas bag, which he caught.

Honest-to-goodness gold coins!

He heard a gunshot, saw a brief red flash, and found himself all muddled again until he pulled himself out of the dirt. Back in the dreary place. Those greyscale people, spread far from each other, labouring. Did they wear robes or dresses? He didn't stop to properly look at them. In front of him was the same grey, crumpled tombstone; the same ground as before. Was this a dream?

Once again, the beanstalk took him. A quick self-inspection revealed that he was unharmed, but now wearing the same light-coloured shirt with darker vest that he'd had in the Western caper. As he stood on floorboards the size of football fields, he saw a massive, crumpled piece of paper rain from above the monolithic writing desk. It hit the floor with the deep thrumming of a colossal impact, though it still had the distinctly sweeping stiffness of paper.

A glistening voice, that same crystalline flow, spoke clearer now: "Why are the magic beans all grey? Should we try bringing them together? They must be so alone…"

The giant rumbled. "Growth is the opposite of loneliness."

Jack wanted to object to that argument. Turning about, he wanted to look for a way up the desk. His search was cut short as he flew down through the stalk again, for all the world like a dust mote drawn by a vacuum.

The next time, he lived happily ever after.

Then he dug himself out of the ground.

"Here lies…"

"Oh, come ON!" Jack said explosively.

This time, when he reached the floorboards, he attacked the giant foot to get the attention of —

— and then he was in a cavern. He was wearing armour, holding a spear. A group with the same gear surrounded him. At one side was a woman with a magic sword and a man in robes who glowed and murmured. Jack and his friends charged into the centre of the cavern. There were great, golden eggs nearby. Ahead of him, his target: an actual, real, definitely existing Dragon!

Fire, everywhere.

Dirt. "Here lies." Beanstalk. Clouds. Floorboards.

Jack ran to one of the crumpled pieces of paper, wasting no time. Perhaps the suit of armour he still wore infused him with a sense of adventure. Regardless, he heaved the crumpled sheet in a roll to the hole. Voices, rumbling and tinkling, exchanged arguments above him. Paper, however, is heavy at such a size. Voices couldn't penetrate the sound barrier of effort.

He did it! Lifting his helmet visor and wiping his brow on the back of a gauntlet, Jack leaned against the balled-up ideas to catch his breath. Then he was sucked, feet first, under the wad of paper. Its weight resisted, so he found himself sieved between the angular ball and the edge of the floorboards.

"Your eye in the sky has been compromised," came a voice from some kind of attachment in Jack's ear. He started. "Huh?"

The voice didn't respond. Jack was wearing tactical gear: buckles, straps, synthetic materials, weapons, and tools. He was kneeling on a tile floor, back braced against a wall, a 9mm pistol in his hands. He knew, for some reason, that it was loaded with sub-sonic rounds and equipped with a silencer.

He went on to victory in several epic gun fights, a fist fight on the back of an alligator, a danger zone of live electrical wires, and a lengthy boat chase during which just about everything exploded. There was a debriefing in transit, and he connected with a woman for celebrations before having to dig himself out of the dirt again. He was still wearing the tactical suit, though he was now unarmed. The suit had been coloured before. He'd have sworn there had at least been some blue in there.

He was black and white again.

The moment the ghostly beanstalk got him to the floorboards in the sky, Jack turned right around and jumped back in. At least he'd be making the choice this time.

He found himself in a bizarrely lengthy experience in which nothing happened for an extraordinarily long time, and yet he was acutely aware of his thoughts, feelings, and sensory experiences. He didn't even remember dying this time, and he was wearing the spattered overalls of a painter.

"Here Lies Jack
At the end of his song"

Well, the cow bit was gone. He was obscurely pleased by that.

This time, he tried toppling the headstone and attacking the spectral beanstalk.

Once more, despite his efforts, he was in the study as large as a landscape. Jack tried running out into the light, shouting and waving his arms, to get the attention of the giant and the harp. "What was that?" came lyrical words. The giant began to move in his seat. Jack's face was a sun-rise of hope.

Before he knew what was happening, he was in a spacecraft.

After a long string of profanity, he pulled himself back together. He was wearing one of those form-fitting duochrome suits that apparently offered far more protec-tion than their appearance would suggest. "What are you looking at?" he said to the crew around him. One of them pressed a symbol on her suit.

"Captain," she said, never taking her eyes from Jack, "we have an ensign showing signs of—"

Jack fled the room — filled with some kind of weird laser engine — before he could hear any more of what she was saying. *I'm taking control of my life if it kills me*! he thought.

They'd had warning, but he remembered his experi-ences from the spy thriller, so he busted out some impres-sive moves to secure the control deck and crash the ship on a nearby moon. Expecting to wake up on his grave again, he was incredulous to discover that he'd survived the crash. He went on to recover the surviving crew of what turned out to be a warship. A galactic something-or-other.

It took work and many arguments before first forging relationships and then a team. From there, he went on to lead an effort to build a liveable colony from the remains of a ship designed to destroy. In a foreign world. He eventually died from the poison of a homicidal plant.

He ran to the labourers. "HELP!" he cried, and they began waving or calling out to each other in order to converge upon him. He arrived at the feet of a woman in a puritanical dress with a cybernetic eye. She was as greyscale as he was. He began with, "What's happening to me!?" and descended into incoherence before they could get him on his feet and snap his panic back into a cogent mind.

"We won't have a lot of time," said a man to the...Jack had to think these words, and couldn't believe himself, but...cyborg Puritan. Not that the man was any different: he was a ninja with a beer belly and a tiny Dragon on his shoulder. All greyscale. The man continued: "The author could use him again at any moment."

Jack, his hope fading, swept the group with his gaze. Almost all of them were mashups, anachronisms, and other odd recombinations. "What's happening?"

"We're sorry, for what it's worth," said the woman before him. "I know this has seemed harsh for you, but the rest of us miss what you have. At least you experience something other than the endless grey of the forgotten."

Jack furrowed his brow and turned to the dad bod ninja. "Help me out here?"

Legitimate melancholy actually weighed the man down as he slowly shook his head. "Maybe it'll be peace for you. A true, clean end. I hope so, for your sake. We've all tried just about everything. The closest we came was one of our own. But he was also forgotten, so though something grew, it didn't get far. But you? Maybe."

Jack was beginning to sweat. But he was surrounded. For the first time since all this madness began, he glanced back at the beanstalk and actually hoped it would pull him away. Naturally, it didn't. His efforts to fight them off lasted all of two strikes; they'd all had fight scenes of their own.

"Why don't we work together!?" he demanded as they dragged him toward an empty grave. "We could study how I'm different! Practice! I could look for things in the stories!"

"We've tried every agreement, every suggestion. They always end up like us." Jack didn't catch who'd said that, but it was a voice from the crowd. It sounded somehow bestial, though he couldn't place why.

"But what will this gain!?"

He was thrown into an open grave, one of the projects the greyscales had been labouring over. With a tone of pity and not a question, the cyborg Puritan replied as she shovelled the first of the dirt upon him:

"How do you break a vicious cycle?"

EPILOGUE?

She stood behind her sister with her hands in her pockets. "Why bother?" she said. "The sky fell, and we lived."

Her sister, named Coral after the colour of her only dress, counted on the wind to carry her voice. She faced the edge of a cliff, the ocean waves beating below, and kept her eyes on her work. There wasn't quite enough sky to cover what it once did, so she was struggling with how to stitch it together. "My fiancé was an astronaut, Keystone. You know that."

"It's better not to worry about before, though. Everybody was right about the end of the world," Keystone thought aloud, "but no one thought it'd all happen. Lost loves, zombies, storms, wars, pandemics…"

"You know I'm not trying to cover up space or hide things with a new sky."

"That's why I'm confused. Won't you miss him if there aren't any stars? There's not even enough new magic left to bring him home. We could start over. We don't need the sky." Keystone was frustrated.

"He didn't have enough food to last this many years."

Her tone was strange. Not logical, but accepting.

"So, it's not about him?"

"Of course not. I miss him. But I miss a lot of things. Remember cheeseburgers? Electricity? Hanging out in the same place for hours, and safely?"

"Everyone put together can't make it better now," Keystone pointed out.

"Not unless they change," Coral agreed.

Author's Note: *This piece was included in* Kit Sora: The Artobiography, *a collection of her stunning photography accompanied by flash fictions. It was an honour to be a part of such a creative and outstanding project, and the book is gorgeous. You should buy the book as now as possible.*

ACKNOWLEDGMENTS

In terms of short stories and flash fiction, this anthology spans the entirety of my early writing career up to and including the year 2021. It's been a bizarre, convoluted, and wonderful journey so far. There are copious quantities of thanks to give out. I don't have the space or the time to give everyone the full extent of the praises they deserve, and I fear my words will fall well short of the mark. My efforts below are not arranged in any particular order because I can't imagine even attempting to rank such a thing.

All of the gratitude to:

The love of my life, Alisha Morrissey. She's been endlessly supportive. A sounding board on many levels, she has helped me through countless personal and professional doubts. Her own professional writing background also powered some of the most useful and constructive feedback I've ever gotten. Check out her work with the marketing business Rogue Penguin Creative, which she co-founded and co-owns. She's challenged me, exposed me to all manner of new ideas and experiences, and fed me some truly magnificent pasta. She helped me overcome (most of) my fear of dogs. We have cats together. She's my favourite. I wouldn't have gotten this far in my writing ambitions without her at my side.

Coffee.

Matthew LeDrew and my friends and colleagues at Engen Books. Matt in particular has encouraged me at great length, and it was on his initiative that I was brought into the fold. I had the privilege of experiencing his debut as a writing instructor and highly recommend his classes. I'm proud to be an Engen author, and it's been a privilege to read, edit, and work with the other writers under its umbrella. For more on Engen Books, check out www.engenbooks.com

Scott Bartlett. A brilliant man and one of my closest friends. He gave me massive amounts of feedback, guidance, advice, and support during a difficult time in my life. His influence was instrumental in my growth as a writer, and he is -- to use one of his favoured terms -- a "hoopy frood." We've had some great times, and I look forward to our next session of *StarCraft*. I found his novel *Taking Stock* to be particularly impressive, and I recommend a peek at his Facebook group (Scott Bartlett's Spacers).

Mandi Coates, who created the outstanding cover art for this collection. Drop everything and go look at it right now. It's awesome, right? She's also a generally fabulous human. Check out her collection, *Tea, Shadows, and Surprises*, from Engen Books. She also has a Facebook page (Mandi Coates - Artist) with many additional goodies.

The Transnational Arts Production (TrAP). Not only was I thrilled and delighted to have been selected for their "All Borders are Temporary" collection, but it was the milestone that really made me believe I had a future in writing. Their work is inspirational and covers a wide swath of artistic influence. For a look at their organization and its works, visit https://trap.no/en/.

Sandbox Gaming, a non-profit organization. They use video-game-themed activities and events to fundraise for and support children's charities that promote play. I have cherished memories and life-long friends — to say nothing of countless fun experiences — because of this magnificent and magnanimous group. I volunteered with them at a time in my life when lying down to give up sounded like a solid plan. The biggest thing SBG gave me was re-kindled hope. They got me back on track for my whole motivation to write: celebrating the magic in the world. Check them out at www.sandboxgaming.org

Video games. An art form that has given me joy as long as I've known it, the video game has been a pivotal interest of mine. I've connected with communities and friends through gaming. More than that, video games taught me important lessons in my youth about patience, hard work, perseverance, and practice — all vital to life as a writer.

The cats: Shagrat, Omar, and Jak Jak. They give me joy and take my snacks, but don't snuggle me enough. Little jerks.

All of the martial arts clubs, instructors, and groups with whom I've trained. Having been part of these groups made me better as a person and as a writer. Of particular note: Dave Jackman's Kenpo, Butactik in Labrador City (under Don Ballard and Guy Savard), Brazilian Jiu-Jitsu (various), Cheng Style Ba Gua Zan Kung Fu (Josh Bachynski), and Kali style Filipino Martial Arts (Momentum Martial Arts; Steve Crewe and Dennis White).

Scott Drover, Michael Drover, and Kyle Mitchell are particularly noteworthy. Many of my best childhood memories come from them, and they played a large part in my inspiration and ambition to become a writer.

Paul Fowler and Lacey Decker. They created Paragon Press. As I mentioned previously, my first-ever published work was included in the debut *Paragon* anthology.

Kieran John Dooley, music given form. We've had many great conversations about art, music, storytelling, human nature, and life. His humanist life philosophy, "Don't be a dick," is pure wisdom. His projects have included Centrefold (https://centrefoldnl.bandcamp.com/), Dora (https://dora.bandcamp.com/), and Hurricane Avenue (https://hurricaneavenue.bandcamp.com/music).

Nick Bruff, fellow writer and metalhead. We have dubbed ourselves the Blood Metal Brothers because we enjoy shenanigans. You might have seen his background performances in Netflix shows like *Frontier* or *Hudson & Rex*. We've thrown up the horns for each other's writing many times, and appreciate the whiskey Writer's Tears because reasons.

Philip Davis. He introduced me to the works of Brandon Sanderson and Patrick Rothfuss, which is enough by itself. A stalwart friend, he has offered ideas, suggestions, and criticisms — to say nothing of exposure to concepts and ideas I hadn't encountered elsewhere. We've absorbed innumerable hours discussing storytelling, reading, writing, and fan communities. In fact, we've talked about all manner of nerdy things while in retail drudgery, and I doubt I'd have lasted so long at the job without those conversations to keep me sane.

Dad (hi, Big Guy!), my stepmother, and my siblings. My grandmother, Uncle Gordon, Aunt Kim, and all the family who played roles — big and small — in my adventures of life and writing.

More awesomeness: Chris Kendall, Darcy Bartlett, the Labrador City Public Library, Ruth Simmons, Katherine Burgess, the A. C. Hunter Public Library, books and bookstores, coffee shops, the Sci Fi on the Rock convention and everyone involved in it, The Ship Pub, LSPU Hall, Memorial University of Newfoundland and Labrador, Donna Walsh, Jennifer Lokash, Danine Farquharson, Mami Kubota, Matthew Howse, Greg Wheeler, Chris Skanes, Chris Ringrose, Kimberly Ringrose, Morgan Smith, my D&D crowds, Rob McDonald, Michele Grant, Emilee Marsh, Robyn Marsh, Delaney Marsh, Maxwell Marsh, Elaine Budgell, Gerald Carew.

BLESSED REST

The railway was an iron border of money. The Fae were struggling to survive.

"Give me wisdom," Carnation pleaded. Her bow, fused and fueled by a legacy of flowers, rested with her as she leaned back her head and closed her eyes. Her breath returned with effort.

"Why do you fight?" asked the Pine.

Her forehead lifted, but she didn't open her eyes. Rest, blessed rest between war machines. "Aren't you with the Winter Court? Why are you speaking to me?"

Pine's voice was between shuddering wind and shivering bark. "Why does a Pale Elf bear Summer's blossoms?"

"Fair enough," Carnation said. If Pine wished to slay her, so be it. Blessed rest.

"You carry a human smell, metallic and greasy. But something else. Are you with child?"

"The train magnate," she said.

Needles of shock. "Would he not have you?"

"He would, and he loves the forest dearly. The Dreaming and the Fair Folk."

"Then why?"

"He belongs to the Iron Court. What could he do?"

"What of the babe?"

"Half of each."

"All of neither."

"Half of neither," Carnation corrected. The flowers of her bow bloomed. Still her eyes were closed. "A child between the two could be a bridge…"

Rustling. "That is a sliver of hope."

One dimple lifted. "Isn't that the human way?"

ABOUT THE AUTHOR

Matthew Daniels is an author currently living in St. John's, Newfoundland.

He has over a dozen writing credits both locally and internationally, and his work had been featured in best-selling anthologies on five separate occasions. Stories include 'Grey Anatomy' in *Paragon*, 'Where With All' in *All Borders are Temporary,* and too many stories to count in the *From the Rock* series.

In December 2019 he was named a member of the Engen Books Board of Directors.

His first novel, *Diary of Knives*, was released in January 2021.

Manufactured by Amazon.ca
Bolton, ON